pH

WORD,
- 10

d paper

C000319906

The Family He Wanted

KAREN SANDLER

MILLS & BOON®

First published in Great Britain 2010
Large Print edition 2010
Harlequin Mills & Boon Limited,
Eton House, 18-24 Paradise Road,
Richmond, Surrey TW9 1SR

© Karen Sandler 2009

ISBN: 978 0 263 22151 0

Printed and bound in Great Britain
by CPI Antony Rowe, Chippenham, Wiltshire

KAREN SANDLER

first caught the writing bug at age nine when, as a horse crazy fourth grader, she wrote a poem about a pony named Tony. Many years of hard work later, she sold her first book (and she got that pony—although his name is Ben). She enjoys writing novels, short stories and screenplays and has produced two short films. She and her husband live in Northern California. You can reach Karen at karen@karensandler.net

To the real "Sam", my dad,
a hero beyond compare.

I love you, Dad!

Chapter One

Eyes burning with exhaustion, butt sore from the long drive, Jana McPartland pulled her ramshackle white sedan up to the security gate of Sam Harrison's Sierra Nevada foothills estate. If Sam had changed the gate code since last year, she was sunk. With her cell phone disconnected and not a pay phone in sight, she'd have to sit out here in the gloomy early January drizzle until he next passed through the gate.

She couldn't make out Sam's house—never

mind that it was the size of Nebraska. The big, white two-story was around a curve of the asphalt-paved drive, hidden by a row of cypress trees. She'd spent a month there last May, right before she became Tony Herrera's assistant at Estelle's House. Sam had gone off on a book tour for his latest crime thriller and had asked Jana to house-sit. Talk about the lap of luxury.

She rolled down the driver's-side window, her arm tiring as the hand crank resisted. She had the security code memorized, but still she pulled out the slip of paper Sam had written it on. She liked seeing that almost illegible cursive, the words *Gate Code* reading more like "Goat Cake." He'd laughed when she'd pointed that out to him, had chucked her under the chin like he had when she'd been ten years old.

She knew that touch had meant way more to her than to him. That was why she'd saved the slip of paper, so she could remember that moment.

Tucking the slip of paper back inside her purse, she punched in the five-digit code. A moment of silence, then the gate mechanism clicked and clacked as it rolled aside. She smiled with relief as she continued up the driveway, the gate shutting again behind her.

As she traveled the last curve of the road, her stomach started a two-step, threatening a redo of the nausea that never seemed limited to the morning. She'd eaten lunch at twelve-thirty in Redding, downed a few crackers when she'd stopped for pee breaks in Corning and Sacramento. The only time her stomach cooperated was while she was eating. At three-thirty, with all the crackers gone, it wasn't looking good.

She tucked the sedan alongside the six-car garage, out of the way in case Sam wasn't here and had to pull in. Even on a nasty, rainy

Friday afternoon, he could be out running errands. Sam had a thing about keeping his six cars out of the elements, especially the five to-drool-for vintage models in his collection.

Her back aching, she unfolded herself from the sedan, brushing cracker crumbs from her elastic-waist jeans. Snagging her thrift shop jacket from the passenger seat, she shoved her arms into the sleeves. Nothing to keep her head dry, but hopefully she wouldn't be out in the wet for very long.

She'd always loved Sam's house—the wraparound front porch shaded with oak trees, the wide front lawn that sloped gently along the drive. She would have killed for a lawn like that as a kid, a place to run, a million nooks and crannies for hide-and-seek. She'd made do with Estelle Beckenstein's tiny front yard and backyard. She'd sneak over there from the small apartment where she and her mom lived, play rough-and-tumble games with Estelle's foster kids. But Sam's sixty-acre estate was a kid's dream.

Relieved to be under the porch overhang, she tried the doorbell first, pressing her ear to the front door to make sure the three-note gong sounded. Then she knocked, just to be on the safe side. Still no response. Of course, if he was out back somewhere, he wouldn't hear the doorbell or her knock.

Walking along the porch, Jana made her way around the house. She could kill two birds here—one, look for Sam, and two, brave the wet to see if he still left the little bathroom out by the pool unlocked. That would save her the indignity of using the bushes. She'd taken care of business at the service station when she eked out another quarter tank with the last of her cash, but that was a good half hour and a soda ago. Caffeine free, of course.

He hadn't locked the bathroom. That gave her a chance to not only use the toilet but also wash her face and finger-comb her stick-straight chin-length hair. That was a laugh, considering the way the damp strands clung to her face. Hopefully, she wouldn't terrify him when he got home.

Nothing to do but wait. Trotting back to the porch as the rain started in earnest, she retraced her steps to the front. He'd added a porch swing out here, giant-size, big enough for even six-foot-four Sam to stretch out on. A blanket lay folded over the back, and the seat was piled high with pillows. It looked too comfy to pass up.

Shucking her wet jacket, she flopped it over the porch rail then sank onto the soft cushions. The swing swayed as she tugged the blanket over her. Warmth suffused her, the patter of rain a pleasant accompaniment to the motion of the swing.

Since the day the test stick turned blue, stark fear had been her constant companion. Sometimes her terror grew so fierce it all but choked her. But now that she was here, safe at Sam's, she could let it go.

A sudden thought speared her mind, wrenched her from her peace. What if Sam was off on another tour? What if he was a thousand miles away from here and out of reach? No phone, her car nearly on empty— what would she do?

Tears ambushed her. Fighting them back, she turned over, burrowing her forehead into the back of the swing. Squeezing her eyes shut, she tightened her hands into fists and pressed them tightly against her chest. She refused to cry. Refused to be all red-eyed when Sam got home.

And he would come home. He had to. Because she needed him. Because she didn't have anywhere else to go.

Water rolling off his high-tech jacket and rain pants, Sam Harrison hiked up the wooded hill behind his house, satisfied he'd cleared enough brush to keep his creek from over-flowing its banks. He'd spent an hour pulling deadfall from the roiling water, hauling soaked branches high enough up the bank to keep them from falling back into the creek. Now when the next storm arrived later tonight, the creek's flow would continue downstream rather than collect at the tight bend behind his house.

Not that the approaching deluge could have dumped enough water to risk flooding his house. It had been built at the top of the rise, well out of the flood zone. But after a rough, wakeful night, his skin had crawled with the kind of toxic, restless energy that severe sleep deprivation always gave him. He'd had to burn it off with something physical.

He'd been all ready to head into town, his power tools loaded into his pickup, gripping the keys to what he privately referred to as his secret folly. He'd told no one about the little storefront in Camino he'd closed escrow on six weeks ago—not his best friend Tony, not his former foster mom Estelle. He feared they'd laugh at his whimsical idea. Even worse, Estelle would know immediately from what sad, wretched place his hare-brained notion to open a Christmas store had come.

It was contemplation of their judgment, as well as the strengthening deluge, that changed his mind. The retrofit of the store could wait for yet another day. He'd be better off with the punishing misery of pulling rain-soaked deadfall out of an icy creek.

Reaching the porch steps, he headed for the back door, then remembered he'd left it locked. He'd have to go around to the front. Which meant he'd have to slip off his muck-covered boots outside the door. He might not give a damn about muddy footprints on the travertine tile entry, but his cleaning lady would have a hissy fit.

About to tug open the screen door, his gaze drifted over to the porch swing, then to the rain pouring buckets beyond it. Then in a double take, he fixed back on the swing. Who the hell was curled up on his cushions, snugged down all comfy and cozy under his blanket?

For a flash of a heartbeat, he wondered if it was Faith, come to beg him to take her back. Except he'd seen the acceptance in her eyes last week when he'd handed over the coup de grâce in the form of a diamond tennis bracelet. Faith had seen it coming. She was good enough friends with one of her predecessors to know how Sam would end it: a pricey gift, a kiss on the cheek, a firm goodbye.

So he wouldn't have the messiness of Faith's return to deal with. He crossed the porch to the swing. It swayed ever so slightly when a gust of wind curled under the overhang and hit it.

The woman had her back to him. She'd buried her face into the swing's cushions as if she'd wanted to close out the world.

With the blanket pulled just past her chin and her light brown hair fallen partway onto her cheek, he couldn't see the woman's face. But something familiar about her tickled the back of his mind.

Could she be a foster kid, someone who knew about his history? Maybe she'd heard about Estelle's House, Tony's independent living program for emancipated fosters. Could be she wanted Sam's help getting a spot at the ranch. But how'd she get past the wrought-iron fence and security gate? She looked far too delicate to have jumped the fence.

Lightning sparked in the sky, and it must have been nearby, because the thunder that followed hit like an explosion. With a gasp, the woman's eyes snapped open, and she jolted upright on the swing. Her gaze locked on him, her brown eyes so huge they seemed to fill her face.

"Sam."

Her voice trickled down his spine. His brain finally engaged. "Jana."

She pushed aside the blanket and fussed with her hair. In quick succession, he registered the changes, the differences that had foiled his recognition of her. No more bleached-blond, pink-streaked hair. Her short, spiky cut had grown out long enough to cover the nape of her neck, its natural honey-brown color reminding him of that pugnacious kid he knew from Estelle's. She hadn't been a foster kid like him, but her mother had neglected her enough that Jana spent more time at Estelle's than she did at home.

Not only her hair but also her body had changed from the tomboyish twenty-three-year-old's he'd known last year. Her face was rounder, her hips a little broader and her breasts—

Okay, better not to think about her breasts. Yeah, he'd noticed around the time Jana turned twenty that she wasn't a little girl anymore. She had a lot less meat on her bones than most of the women he dated, but her lean-as-a-racehorse body nevertheless intrigued him. But she was a friend and he'd known her since she was a child. Breasts shouldn't even be in his lexicon with Jana, even though the ratty blue V-neck sweater she wore shaped them so nicely.

He dragged his gaze back up to her face. "You came back." Nothing like stating the obvious.

His staring must have made her jittery, because she jumped to her feet. She went green the moment her sneakers hit the deck, clutching the chain suspending the porch swing and swaying with its motion. He grabbed her, hooking her arm around his waist and supporting her across her shoulders.

"Let's get inside," he said as he walked her

to the door. She leaned against him, damp but warm, softer in places he remembered being bonier.

As they crossed the entryway—so much for keeping his cleaning lady happy—Jana tried to wriggle away from him. "I'm fine. Let me go."

"You looked ready to pass out a minute ago."

"Just let me sit." She glanced down at his feet. "Mrs. Prentiss will go ballistic if you walk on her carpet with those muddy boots."

"It's my carpet. I can walk on it any way I want."

Jana lifted one brow. "She scares you spitless. You lock yourself up in your office when she comes to clean."

"I'm just trying to stay out of her way."

Jana smirked and he knew he'd lost the argument. It was only a few steps from the entry to the recliner anyway. She made the short trip without incident and eased herself into the chair.

Hooking his jacket on the coatrack, he bent to unlace the offending boots. "Can I get you something?"

The leather upholstery creaked as she reclined. "Some saltines. I'll get them myself. After the month I spent house-sitting, I probably know better than you where to find them."

He was contemplating the fact that she probably was right when a game show ding-ding-ding went off in his head. Despite his chosen career as a novelist, he'd always had a fair mind for math. He could generally add two and two and come up with the correct answer.

He listed the clues mentally. The soft rounding of Jana's body. Her obvious nausea when she stood too fast. The request for saltines.

He skimmed off his rain pants and tucked his long-sleeved henley more securely into his jeans. "You stay put. I'll get them." He marched off to the kitchen, catching himself worrying whether his damp socks would leave prints on the carpet.

Stepping inside the walk-in pantry, he started scanning the groaning shelves arranged in a U around the narrow space. When Jana spoke behind him, he nearly jumped out of his socks.

"I've seen mini-marts with less merchandise."

He turned and found her inches away, leaning to one side to see past him. "Don't you ever listen to what you're told?"

"Where's the fun in that?" She edged around him toward the bottom of the U, smelling of rain-dampened flowers. "Does Mrs. Prentiss still alphabetize everything?"

"She doesn't alphabetize." Trying to shake her scent loose, he backed away and came up hard against a shelf full of pasta. "She just organizes it to make it easier for me to make a meal."

"Like boxed mac and cheese or canned chili? There they are."

She went up on tiptoe to snag the saltines from the top shelf. But the shelf heights accommodated his six-foot-four frame, not Jana's five-six height. Wannabe five-footer Mrs. Prentiss used a stepladder to off-load groceries onto the highest shelves.

All Jana managed to accomplish was another apparent bout of dizziness that tipped her toward him. Her hands slapped against his chest for balance as he gripped her shoulders. He had a three-second grace period to enjoy the feel of her hands clutching his henley before he got a good look at her face. This time she was even greener about the gills.

As she sagged against him, he lifted her carefully into his arms. She whacked him on the chest and said feebly, "Put me down."

He kept walking out to the living room. "I'd just as soon you not upchuck on my floor."

Her throat worked as she swallowed. "I might do the honors on your shirt."

He put her on the sofa, then emptied the small plastic wastebasket Mrs. Prentiss kept tucked under an end table. He thrust the wastebasket into Jana's hands. "Be right back with the crackers."

His stocking feet nearly went out from under him when he hit the kitchen, the slippery tile color-coordinated to the travertine entryway. Snatching up the saltines, he retraced his steps, then stopped short in the doorway as the sound of Jana being sick reached his ears.

If he knew Jana, the last thing she'd want would be a witness to her indignity. Cracker box tucked under his arm, he went back into the kitchen, tore a couple paper towels off the roll and wet them at the sink. Then he brought the towels and saltines out to Jana.

Lolling against the sofa back with her eyes shut, she had the wastebasket propped on her knees. He took it without comment, handing her the paper towels and dropping the crackers on the coffee table, then took the mess to the guest bathroom for cleanup. When he returned, she was swiping her face with the towel.

"You want to rinse your mouth?" She nodded in response to his query. "Can you make it to the bathroom?" Another nod.

He helped her to her feet; then when she shook off his hand, he let her go on her own speed to the bathroom. She walked the short distance carefully, as if she expected the floor to tilt at any moment.

If not for the math he'd done earlier, Jana's illness would have worried him. Not that he wasn't wrestling with some class-A anxiety, considering the likely reality of her situation, but he'd had a little prep on just this kind of female condition. Tony had just regaled him about how his wife, Rebecca, had had her first bout of morning sickness just last weekend. Sam would have begged off on hearing all the gory details, but he knew how excited the couple were about the baby.

When Jana emerged from the bathroom, she didn't look much more cheerful, but her color was a little better. The problem was, instead of letting her flop onto the sofa, he wanted to pull her back into his arms, cradle her on his lap. Maybe even press a kiss against her forehead.

What the hell was wrong with him? Faith's departure, never mind that he instigated it, must have impacted him worse than he'd thought. Otherwise he wouldn't be entertaining such crazy ideas about Jana.

He waited until she'd seated herself cross-legged on the sofa, then took the recliner for himself. She scooped the box of crackers from the table and took her time tearing open the end flap. She took the same deliberate care in ripping open the packet of saltines.

A cracker in her hand, she eyed him warily. "I'm pregnant."

"So I gathered." He helped himself to a cracker. Just to be sociable, not because he could brush her fingers in the process. "So where's Ian? I presume he's the proud papa."

"Not so proud." She finished her cracker and plucked out another. "When he got the news, he left skid marks in the carpet while running out the door." Her laugh was hollow. "Believe it or not, neither one of us had ever been with anyone else. I guess he couldn't handle hitting the jackpot with his first relationship."

A compulsion filled Sam to pound the feckless boy into the ground. He tended to limit homicide to the pages of his books, but he could make an exception for Ian.

With an effort, he kept his tone light. "So you got tired of Portland, Oregon, and came home."

"It was either that or live in my car." She smiled, but he didn't miss the desperation in her brown eyes. "The pub I was working at closed.

Couldn't afford the apartment without Ian. Not that he was helping a whole heck of a lot."

Sam's murderous impulse transformed into an icy rage. He remembered Ian as a bit of a slacker, mid-twenties with no discernible goals in sight. Maybe not one hundred percent dependable, but to cut and run, leaving Jana holding the bag, was despicable.

"Any idea where he is now?" Sam asked, teeth clenched, jaw aching.

"Not a clue. Midwest somewhere? Maybe back with his family in Indiana." Second cracker finished, she set aside the packet and fixed her gaze on him. "I'm dead broke, Sam, and in big trouble. A buck-fifty in my pocket, two months pregnant and sick as a dog."

His heart squeezed tightly in his chest. Over the fourteen-plus years he'd known her, she had asked him for almost nothing. Even now, she was hanging tough, doing her best to hide the panic that seeped around the edges. But she was all but on her knees here. And she'd come to him. Not Tony, not Estelle or Rebecca. Him.

It took almost more willpower than he possessed to resist throwing his arms around her. That kind of sappy comforting would only acknowledge that he saw her weakness. So he stayed in his chair, linking his hands in his lap to keep from reaching for her.

"What is it you need?" he asked.

She hunched in on herself a little bit. "After the way I walked out on Tony, left him in the lurch…" The first threads of tears stitched her words. "I just can't face him on my own. I thought if you went with me, talked to Tony, he'd give me my job back. Give me a place to stay."

"With the Estelle's House program." A stone settled in the pit of his stomach. "At the ranch."

Hope lit her face. "I'll bunk with one of the

students if I have to. Take a cut in pay. Anything."

"Jana." He did take her hand then. "There have been some changes since you left. The work you were doing…the kids do that now. Rebecca's taking care of fund-raising. Estelle fills in as needed. Your job is gone."

"But I could stay at the ranch… Maybe find a job in town…"

"Every bed is filled, and then some. Estelle's sharing with Ruby in the main house. There'd be no place to put you."

Her eyes welled; her hand trembled. "Sam, I've got nowhere else to go." Tears spilled down her cheeks.

Shaking her head in denial, she yanked her hand free and jumped to her feet. Swiping the wetness from her eyes, she took off across the foyer, fumbling for her purse, groping for the door. He caught her before she could turn the knob.

At first she resisted, slapping his chest to get free of him. Then she tumbled into his arms and sobbed her heart out.

God, he wanted to bottle her pain and throw it far out into the ocean. Where he'd felt maybe an ounce of sympathy for Faith when she'd opened that jewelry box, he staggered under the weight of Jana's sorrow. Where he wouldn't in a million years want Faith back, he overflowed with gratitude that this quirky, wise-mouthed friend had returned home.

"We'll work it out, kid," he murmured. "We'll find a way to make it right."

Chapter Two

Jana didn't know why she'd expected anything different, considering the hell-in-a-handbasket mode her life had been in the past couple months. Really, it had been all downhill since she'd walked out on Tony and the Estelle's House program last Labor Day weekend to run off with Ian. Of the four months since then, she'd had maybe one good week before her rat boyfriend showed his true, lazy colors.

This was no way to start her homecoming,

no matter how good it felt to have Sam's arms around her. She had to claim some space, get her head clear so she could figure out what the heck she'd do next. She'd never manage it with Sam thinking he had to save her just like his Trent Garner character would save the world in one of his thriller novels.

Palms pressed against Sam's chest, she pushed away from him, closing her mind to the feel of hard muscle under soft knit. He'd hugged her plenty of times, when she was a skinny ten-year-old brat, when she was a hormone-crazed teen, and more recently during those far-and-few-between visits he made to the ranch. She'd felt nothing but kindness in the gesture all these years, never mind how she'd fantasized about something more when she was a starry-eyed sixteen-year-old and he was twenty-seven. She'd given up that adolescent dream years ago. She reminded herself that now, just as he had then, he just wanted to comfort her.

Feeling as wrung out as a tatty old rag, she returned to the sofa and collapsed into its deep cushions. Her mind was numb with exhaustion. She had to figure out what to do next, but she didn't have the energy to put two brain cells together.

She scrubbed at her face. "If you could just give me a few minutes, I'll get out of your way."

He switched on a table lamp, illuminating the storm-darkened living room. God, he looked good, even in holey jeans and a plain knit shirt, his overlong hair in need of a good cut.

Sitting in the recliner, he leaned toward her, elbows on his knees, large hands linked. "It's pouring rain. Not exactly traveling weather."

"I'll figure out something." She wanted so much to take his hand, hold tight against the torrent inside her.

"When are you due?" he asked quietly.

"End of July." Seven long months filled with a thousand unknowns waiting to trip her up.

"And then?" he asked.

This was the place she didn't like going to. Because it stole her breath, stabbed her heart with hot regret. Unplanned or not, fathered by a jerk or not, this was beyond unbearable.

She tried to say it as if it were a matter of little concern, except it tore her voice into shreds. "Then I give the baby up for adoption."

She waited for him to argue with her. Tell her she was a terrible person to give her baby away. She glanced over at him sidelong when he didn't speak. "I have to. I'm twenty-four years old. No job, no money, no education. I can't support a child."

He continued to stare at her for long silent moments. Outside, the wind picked up, howling through the trees. A dark, lonely sound.

Finally, he spoke. "If you think it's best, for you and the baby, that's what you should do."

His acceptance of her decision only made her feel worse. The thought of pushing to her feet, walking out the door and to her car utterly overwhelmed her. She'd left her jacket on the porch rail. It would be soaked by now. No protection against the deluge.

Nevertheless, she reached down deep for the strength to get up. Might have made it if not for one large hand closing around hers, keeping her on the sofa.

"You're not going out in that," he told her. When she would have protested, he put a finger to her mouth. "You're staying here, in the downstairs bedroom. Tomorrow morning, we'll figure out what happens next."

She tried not to focus on where he was touching her. The warm contact took her mind on a one-way trip to crazy. "It's my mess, Sam. I have to be the one to take care of it."

"I'm just giving you a place to sleep tonight,

not a solution to your problems. You're welcome to work that out on your own."

Except even as Sam said it, Jana could just about see the wheels turning in his head. He was a rescuer, had been since he was a boy, according to Estelle. He'd bring home stray dogs, lost kittens. As an adult, he gave buckets of money to Tony's independent living program, helping Tony rescue aged-out foster kids instead of cuddly kittens.

She was pretty sure that somewhere in that awesome brain, he was ticking away, coming up with a way to save her from herself. It was tempting to let him—she knew she was just as much a first-class screwup as her mom. But her mother, who had flitted from one crisis to the next, waiting for some man to fall at her feet and fix everything, had been beautiful and a born charmer. Jana had no illusions she had the womanly wiles to lure any man.

Jana pulled free, unfolding herself from the

sofa. Immediately light-headed, she teetered, falling against the rock that was Sam. He actually picked her up in his arms again, just like in his book *Crash* when Trent Garner swept the heroine off her feet to save her from the bad guys. Except the heroine wasn't mortified the way Jana was. Probably didn't feel like upchucking either.

He carried her to the downstairs bedroom and laid her on the bed. Level and motionless, she managed to ward off the nausea. Last thing she wanted was a repeat of her earlier indignity.

He pulled off her still-damp sneakers, then covered her with the comforter folded at the foot of the bed. "Take a nap. We'll talk about this when you wake up."

She wanted to argue the point, would have if she could have kept her stomach under control. Not to mention that when she started feeling cozy under the thick comforter, her eyes got so heavy she didn't have a prayer of keeping them open. She'd have to let him win this one. She could leave later, when she was rested. Walk out to the car and say her goodbyes. Later…

Sam waited until her breathing grew even and deep and her body relaxed. Then he left her, reckoning the more distance he put between them the better. She'd felt too damn good cradled in his arms when he'd carried her, her hair sweetly scented by the rain, her body warm against his. When he started contemplating pulling off her jeans—because they were damp and mud-splattered—he knew he had no business staying in that room.

He had to keep her here, at least for the night. She wasn't an idiot and would probably see the logic of putting off her next steps until the weather cleared. If she gave him guff, he'd call Estelle and let her talk some sense into Jana.

Maybe if he brought her things into the house, that would be an extra inducement to stay. She'd want to change out of her damp, muddy clothes anyway. With any luck, she'd left her little Honda Civic unlocked so he could carry in her suitcase and whatever.

Of course, it could be she had her keys stuffed in the pocket of her jeans and he might be able to fish them out without waking her. His mind fixated on that possibility, displaying a full-color video of him reaching under those warm covers, fingering his way inside her pocket.

He clamped a lid on those images, marching himself over to the entryway for his boots and rain gear. Outside, he circled around to the far side of the garage and stared in confusion at the battered white sedan there. What happened to the late model red Civic she'd left here in last September? He'd cosigned the loan to help her buy it, and she'd been damn proud of the car.

Had she wrecked it? His stomach clenched at the thought of her being in an accident, especially in her current condition.

At least the beater was unlocked. During a quick look through the passenger cabin, he didn't find much. A sweater and a pair of sandals were tossed on the backseat alongside a half-dozen scattered paperbacks—all of them his books. All of them dog-eared, likely from multiple readings.

A plastic market bag under the driver's seat gave him a place to stash the books, sweater and shoes. He popped the trunk and found a small duffel bag, an even-smaller cosmetic bag and a box filled with books. A DVD with a cracked case was wedged in the box—an adaptation of his first novel and his favorite of the six that had made it into film.

The day he'd received his prerelease copy of the movie from his agent, he'd taken it to Estelle's. A rainy Saturday afternoon in

February. Jana was there, helping Estelle ride herd on three new foster girls as they cleaned house.

Jana, fourteen and skinny as a rail, had wise-cracked that the lead actor wore a toupee and she hoped he didn't lose it in the action scenes. But when they'd all sat down to watch it, she'd been enthralled, grabbing his hand during the high climax, holding on so tightly he'd thought his fingers would pop off.

When the movie had officially came out on DVD, he'd given her a copy, had autographed the cover. She'd made a smart remark about how much she might be able to get for it at a flea market, but she'd hung on to it these past ten years. That it meant so much to her, that maybe she even treasured it, set off an ache, an emotion inside him he didn't even want to name.

With market bag and duffel hooked on his fingers, cosmetic bag on top of the box of books, he elbowed the trunk shut and hurried toward the house. If not for the books, she could have fit everything in a paper shopping bag, the luggage of choice for a foster kid. She hadn't experienced that transient, unpredictable life as he had. She'd had a mother, no matter how undependable. But he'd ended up living on a sixty-acre estate, while it seemed Jana still hadn't found her way.

She wasn't his responsibility. She was a close friend, and he did everything he could for good friends. But that didn't mean he should step into her business and try to make everything better.

Back in the house, he set aside the small pile of Jana's worldly goods and stripped off his now-soaked boots, jacket and rain pants. The quiet told him Jana was likely still sleeping, but he nevertheless checked on her. She'd rolled on her side, her silky hair just long enough to spill across her eyes. He itched to smooth it back, but besides the fact that it would tick her off if he touched her while she slept, he couldn't risk waking her when she so obviously needed her rest.

Backing from the bedroom, he climbed the stairs to the second floor. His office overlooked the slope leading down to the creek; with the windows open, he could hear the rush of water below. Oaks, pines and cedars crowded the banks on either side, red-barked manzanita filling the spaces in between. Sometimes, when he drew a blank on what dark hellhole to next send Trent Garner into, he'd gaze out the windows, watch hawks circle in the sky or deer leap through the trees.

Sitting at his desk, he punched in Tony's number. Rebecca answered, laughter in her voice. "Estelle's House."

"It's Sam."

She giggled, then whispered, "Tony, stop it," before returning to the phone. "Sorry,

Sam. Tony's not behaving. I'm guessing it's him you want to talk to."

As she handed over the phone, he heard more laughter, then more scolding before Tony came on the line. "How's it going?" Tony asked, his happiness evident in his voice. Tony's life had been one hard-luck story after another, but since his and Rebecca's remarriage and her pregnancy, he was a changed man.

Sam had no right feeling any kind of envy for his friend. Sam had a hundred times more than many people had—a burning hot career as a thriller novelist, a gorgeous home, a garage full of high-ticket automobiles. His pick of women. But sometimes Sam felt he'd give anything for Tony's riches—his wife, Rebecca; his five-year-old daughter, Lea; and their baby-to-be.

"Sam?" Tony prodded.

Sam returned his attention to the phone. "A little something has come up. Jana's back."

A few moments of silence ticked away. "How is she?"

"Pregnant." He told Tony the rest of it, how she'd turned up on his doorstep with barely more than a junker car and the clothes on her back.

"Where's Ian?" Tony asked.

"The father of the year is AWOL. She was hoping I could intervene to get her position back at the ranch." Before Tony could state the obvious, Sam added, "I told her how things have changed."

"You know I'd help her if I could," Tony said. "But once they all arrive, we'll have double the participants we had the first session. There'll be students stuffed away in every nook and cranny on the ranch."

"We could build another modular." They'd added two to the property when they ran out of space in the existing structures.

"To be honest, I don't think the teens in the

program can stand the disruption. They've been arriving since the day after Christmas, a tough time of the year for any foster."

Sam had lived that heartbreak, had the scars to prove it. Before he could stop himself, his mind drifted to his secret folly, the Christmas shop. In his imagination, it was filled to the rafters with glittering ornaments and decorated trees. A tree for every year after his mother left.

Sam shut the door on the past as Tony snagged his focus again. "Not to mention Becca's pregnancy just about has her whipped."

"No worries. Jana's safe here for the moment."

He said his goodbyes, then listened again for any sign that Jana was stirring. All quiet below. At loose ends, he went through his e-mail, replied to a query from his agent about a radio interview, skimmed several dozen notes from fans. Three were from aspiring writers he'd met at conferences or signings, and he felt a twinge of guilt that he hadn't yet replied.

His agent had suggested he hire an assistant, but that was another to-do he'd yet to cross off his list. He didn't like the thought of letting someone into as intimate a part of himself as his writing life. How could he trust handling his fans to a total stranger?

The idea that blindsided him was so brilliant he felt like a doofus for not thinking of it sooner. Who could he better trust than Jana? She already knew the stories of some of the budding writers he was mentoring—the twenty-two-year-old kid whose raw talent had knocked Sam's socks off, the seventysomething grandma who'd written a devious and hilarious cozy mystery.

Could he persuade her to take the job? It wasn't really full-time work, and even a fair wage wouldn't be enough to live on. Maybe if he padded her salary…

Outside, the drenched day had darkened to black. He wandered back downstairs to see what he could scare up for dinner. The doorway to the room where Jana slept might as well have been a magnet, pulling him off his intended path. He only lingered there a few moments, watching her chest rise and fall, thanking God she was here and safe.

His quick scan of the refrigerator told him what it usually did—that he didn't know a damn thing about cooking. Rebecca, Tony's wife and the head cooking instructor at Estelle's House, could throw together a feast using air and fairy dust. His lone specialty was scrambled eggs and toast. Maybe if he added sliced oranges like they did at restaurants, he could call it a complete meal.

He laid out the eggs, bread and fruit on the granite-topped island, then checked the clock. Five-thirty. Should he wake Jana? Let her sleep herself out?

On his way back to the living room, the phone ringing made the decision for him. He dove for the handset on the coffee table, but there was little chance the bedroom extension hadn't rung in Jana's ear. Then it turned out to be a wrong number.

As he set down the phone, Jana emerged, sleepy-eyed, from the bedroom. Her pale blue sweater was rucked up on one side, revealing nothing more than the elastic waist of her jeans. He imagined sliding the hem up that one more inch necessary to bare her smooth skin.

Then she tugged the sweater down, and he gave himself a mental slap. "Are you hungry?"

"Sick as a dog," she said. "Which means I better eat. That's the only time I feel human."

Her attention strayed to the pile of belongings he'd arranged beside the entryway. Color rose in her cheeks, anger and shame warring in her face. "What are you doing bringing my things in here?"

"I wasn't sure what you'd need, so I just brought it all."

"I never said I was staying." She strode across the living room to the entryway. "Did you go through it all?"

He could feel heat rise in his face even though he hadn't touched a thing. "I just carried it from the car. What happened to the Honda?"

She zipped open her duffel, pushed aside the clothes piled on top. "I let Ian talk me into selling it for some extra cash."

He caught a glimpse of a stack of papers held together with a rubber band in the duffel. Then she dropped a pair of skimpy red panties onto the tiled entryway, short-circuiting his brain. The image of Jana in those panties played out in Technicolor in his mind.

Faith had only been gone a week. Between his travel, her travel and the writing on the wall, it had been at least a month since they'd slept together. Was he that sex-deprived to be lusting after Jana? When she'd been nothing but a buddy to him before now?

With barely a glance at them, Jana stuffed the panties back in the duffel and thankfully out of sight. Taking her time, she got to her feet, duffel hooked over her shoulder. She snagged the cosmetics bag with her other hand. She looked ready to walk out the door.

He stepped into her path. "Don't be stupid, just because I pissed you off."

For a moment she looked as if she wanted to blast him. But then she took a breath, her chin tipping up in defiance. "I'll stay. But just for tonight." Shoulders flung back, cosmetic bag and duffel clutched to her chest, she snatched the packet of crackers from the coffee table and retreated into the bedroom.

Once she'd shut the door behind her, Jana tossed the duffel onto the bed and grabbed a handful of crackers. Stuffing a saltine into her mouth, she ferried the cosmetic bag to the adjacent bathroom. She was pretty desperate for food, but a hot shower sounded too good to pass up, especially since Sam had brought in a change of clothes for her. The crackers would tide her over.

Thank God he hadn't seen the letters. She'd managed to hold on to them for ten-plus years, had kept them safe from Ian's prying eyes for four months. Not an easy task when her donkey butt boyfriend wasn't the least ashamed of opening her mail or digging through her dresser drawer in search of a check or some ready cash.

The duffel had a reinforced bottom that lifted out; she slipped the letters underneath for more security. Good thing she hadn't left them under the seat or Sam might have found them when he did his Trent Garner-style search of her car. Bad enough he saw she'd saved the movie and every autographed book he'd ever given her.

Despite the beginnings of queasiness, the hot

shower felt amazing. She scrubbed herself twice, squeezing out every last drop of shampoo to make sure her hair was squeaky clean. Ian always had dibs on the shower before her, and by the time she had gotten in, there was never anything left but lukewarm water.

Wrapping herself in a thick bath sheet with another towel around her head, she knelt to search the cabinet for the hair dryer. There had been one in here when she'd house-sat last May, although as short as her hair was then, she'd never used it. Sam must have moved it.

Padding barefoot through the bedroom, she cracked open the door and called out, "Sam."

Music blasted from the kitchen, the Eagles rocking out a song about heartache. Wasn't that the story of her life.

Sam must not have heard her over Glen Frey. She edged out the door, gripping the bath sheet more tightly. The towel on her head slipped, falling to her shoulders, then to the floor.

She stopped about halfway to the kitchen and shouted over the din of the music. "Sam!" When there was still no response, she filled her lungs with air for another try.

She screamed his name just as he switched off the music. An instant later, Sam came flying out of the kitchen. Closing the space between them, he threw his arms around her and pulled her off her feet.

Flinging her hands out for balance, she lost her grip on the bath sheet. Now the only thing holding it up was the pressure of his body against hers.

Chapter Three

Well, wasn't this an adolescent boy's fantasy. Except he was twenty years past that overheated time of life and the fragrant, delectable female in his arms was Jana. Pregnant, good-buddy-and-not-his-girlfriend Jana.

He started to release her, but she tightened her hold on him. "Wait," she gasped. "The towel."

A downward glance revealed the source of her distress. The bath sheet had loosened, and now hung precariously just above her breasts. Or rather, just above that part of her breasts that had likely hooked it and slowed its descent.

Damn it, don't think about her nipples. Except that was all he could think about now.

"I'll close my eyes," he told her, "and you can fix it."

He not only closed them, he covered them with his hands. He waited as he heard her shift, then walk away from him, presumably in the direction of the bedroom.

"Okay," she said, sounding breathless. She stood in the bedroom doorway, half-hidden by the door.

"When you yelled like that, I thought something bad had happened."

Her cheeks, already red, flamed even brighter. "I just needed the hair dryer. You used to keep it under the sink."

"Faith took it when we split."

"Faith?" she asked. "What happened to Shawna?"

"She left," he said cautiously.

Jana's gaze narrowed on him. "You mean you showed her the door. Like Cyndy. And Patricia. What'd you give Shawna? The emerald choker? Or the tennis bracelet?"

His cheeks burned. "There's another hair dryer in my room. I'll get it for you."

He took the stairs two at a time, feeling as if he was out-running every one of Jana's unspoken accusations. He didn't know why it was any of her damn business how many girl-friends he'd sent packing. As long as it wasn't her he was kicking to the curb.

He stumbled in his bedroom doorway, knees weak at the thought of sending Jana away. She was the only one in his life, Tony and Estelle included, that he felt he could tell just about anything to. Which was why she had an inventory of every girlfriend to whom he'd bid au revoir.

He stared at himself in the bathroom mirror,

wincing against the glare of the track lighting. He just wasn't ready to settle down. Yeah, he was thirty-five, past the age that many men married. But with Shawna, Patricia, Cyndy and Faith, with all their predecessors, he'd start sensing their first steps over that invisible line. The one between fun and games and commitment. And inside him a door would slam shut. Then it was time to call his jeweler.

Digging out the hair dryer from the back of one of the bathroom cabinets, he carried it downstairs. Jana was still waiting by the door, shivering a little.

She snatched the hair dryer from him and shut the door with a muffled "Thanks."

Sam returned to the kitchen. He switched on the Eagles again but toned down the volume. The eggs were cracked in a bowl and ready to scramble, the oranges sliced and ready to put on the plates. Digging around in the freezer, he'd unearthed the chocolate cake he'd tried to forget was there. No reason he and Jana couldn't enjoy it tonight, he'd thought as he'd set it out on the counter to defrost.

Jana's fragrance seemed to drift in before she did. In her stocking feet, she wore another pair of jeans and a pink sweatshirt with a surly looking pig on the front. The slogan across the shirt read Give Me the Latte and Nobody Gets Hurt.

She caught him reading it. "Thrift store. I gave up caffeine when the stick turned blue."

"Have a seat. I'll scramble the eggs."

She tore a slice of bread in two and inhaled half of it. Mouth full, she held up a finger to stop him, then went to the refrigerator. She collected a block of cheese, some tomatoes and an onion. In a quick circuit of the kitchen, she pulled a grater from the cupboard, unhooked a frying pan from its wrought-iron hanger and set the pan on the stove. With a flick of her wrist, she splashed olive oil into the pan and twisted on the gas.

She slapped the cheddar and the grater into his hands. "Shred it, Dano."

Before he could figure out which end of the grater to use, she was chopping the onion and dicing the tomato. The onion fell into the pan with a sharp sizzle, filling the kitchen with an incredible aroma.

Sam juggled the grater and block of cheddar with much less grace. "Looks like you picked up a few tricks from Rebecca." Tony's wife taught kitchen skills as part of the independent living program.

"A few." Jana glanced at him over her shoulder as she flipped the browning onions in the pan. "But I cooked for my mother more often than she cooked for me. It was a matter of survival."

A respectable pile of golden shreds had accumulated on the cutting board and he'd only nicked himself twice. "This enough?" he asked.

She set the frying pan on the granite countertop. "Looks good. Grab me one of those small cereal bowls."

He turned to the cupboard, staring in indecision. "Which ones are cereal bowls?" Behind him, Jana laughed, her amusement putting a smile on his own face even though the joke was at his expense.

"You don't ever use your own kitchen, do you?"

"I nuke stuff in the microwave sometimes. I know where the forks are." He opened a cupboard at random and found neat rows of water glasses. Next door were platters the size of Alaska and bowls big enough to bathe in.

"To your left. No, farther left."

He finally put his hand on the requested item and set it on the counter. She scraped the cooked onions into it, then returned the pan to the stove.

As the oil heated up again, she nibbled on

the rest of the slice of bread. "You can start the toast."

"Finally, something I'm competent at."

She laughed again, and the light in her eyes stole the breath from his lungs. Something burned in his chest; he couldn't tell if it was pain or joy. Either way, he knew it was trouble. Thank God this was just Jana and not a member of his girlfriend parade.

As she poured the scrambled eggs into the hot oil, he kept his attention on the four-slice toaster, lowering the bread, fidgeting with the doneness knob. Anything to stuff down those baffling feelings toward Jana that kept wanting to bubble up.

As he buttered the first of the four slices, Jana tossed cheese, onions and tomatoes into the pan. "Plates in the same cupboard as the bowls."

"I knew that." He set two out onto the counter for her. Using the spatula, she cut the perfect golden omelet in two and served up half on each plate. Sam added the toast and orange circles.

They took their plates to the breakfast nook, a half-octagonal room walled with windows. It was dead-black night out now, nothing visible beyond the white rail of the wrap-around porch.

Jana settled in her chair with a sigh, grabbing a slice of toast even as she scooted toward the table. "I forgot milk. I'm supposed to have at least one glass a day."

"I'll get it." Two months pregnant and she'd made dinner for him. The least he could do was bring her something to drink.

He set two glasses of milk on the table, then took his first bite of omelet. "I think I've died and gone to heaven."

"Just eggs and cheese, Sam." But she seemed pleased by the compliment, which set off that glow inside him again.

He directed his thoughts back to the brilliant idea that had visited him earlier. "I think I have the answer to both our problems."

She swallowed a mouthful of omelet. "You have a problem?"

Certainly not one he'd given much thought to until this evening. "You could work as my assistant. Respond to e-mail, get me organized. Make my travel plans, my appointments."

"I thought you already hired an assistant."

"I never got around to it." He scraped his fingers through his hair, the overgrown length of it irritating him. "I get a million e-mail messages every day that need dealing with, a big stack of letters every week."

She gave him an assessing look. "You desperately need a haircut."

"See what I mean? I never remember to call the stylist. You could go through my e-mail, sort it all out for me. Tell me what I should deal with personally, handle the stuff

I don't need to. It's plenty of work. You'd earn your salary."

Her gaze narrowed. "How much?"

Feeling like a deer in the headlights, he blurted out a figure. Her jaw dropped; then anger flashed in her eyes. "That's too much."

"It isn't the only work I want you to do for me." The words spilled out in a rush.

There was no missing the suspicion in Jana's face. "You're making this up as you go along, aren't you?"

Heat rose in his cheeks. "Not all of it."

"My life isn't one of your books, Sam. You can't just write me into your stories."

Damn straight. The characters in his stories were much better behaved than Jana.

So what else could he have her do? What would keep her busy enough to satisfy her pride, so she'd be willing to let him pay her what he wanted to pay her?

The notion that coalesced in his mind didn't

seem nearly as brilliant. Because it pried open a door he still wasn't ready to crack, even for Jana.

But as he rolled it around, he had to admit it was probably an ideal solution. Flicking a glance at Jana, he took the leap. "There's a project I've been working on."

Her plate clean, she leaned back in her chair, nibbling the last triangle of toast. "A writing project?"

He shook his head. "I bought a storefront in Camino. A gift shop, pretty successful until the owner got sick. It's a wreck now, needs a ton of work before it can open again."

"You're going to run a gift shop?" She swiped her mouth with a paper napkin, missing a crumb of toast. His mind temporarily jumped the tracks as he contemplated brushing that crumb from her bottom lip.

He shifted his brain back into gear. "I thought that eventually the Estelle's House kids can run it. For now, you could help me get it ready. Supervise the foster teens when they come into the picture."

She nodded. "Sounds good. Gives them experience in a different kind of business than food service."

Her approval warmed him, but now came the dicey part. In all the heart-to-hearts he'd had with Jana, he'd managed to omit any details of his time before he arrived at Estelle's. No one but Estelle knew about how his world had ended that December night.

He looked at Jana sidelong, not wanting to face her. Just in case she laughed. "I was thinking of turning it into a Christmas store. You know, Christmas decorations available year-round."

Her brow furrowed. "Just Christmas stuff?"

Defensiveness put an edge on his tone. "I like Christmas. Lots of people like Christmas."

"Sure they do. Me, too. Still…"

Was she going to press him? Ask him to explain? Well, he wasn't going there, not even with Jana.

She gazed at him thoughtfully, then set her crumpled napkin on the plate. "Even if I worked for you, I can't stay here."

He let out a breath he hadn't even realized he was holding. "You wouldn't have to. There's a small apartment above the shop. Needs work, too, so you would have to bunk here for a few days until we could get it livable. But it's got a small kitchen, a bathroom, sleeping area."

She nodded. "That could work."

Relief and anxiety warred within him. As glad as he was that she was considering staying in the area and working for him, he was already regretting the impulse to include her in the plans for the shop. Until now, he could have backed out on the idea any time. Now he felt committed.

He shoved back his chair, grabbed their plates and empty glasses. He slotted the plates and glasses into the dishwasher. "You could stay there rent-free, plus I'd pay you."

Leaning against the dishwasher, hands gripping the cold edge of the granite counter-top, he watched her. In that moment, he wasn't even sure if he wanted her to say yes or no. After all, they could find her an apartment in Sacramento, and he could help her with the rent. His friend Darius, a private investigator, could maybe come up with some busy work for her in his Sacramento office. Darius ran a small operation, with only one investigator besides himself, but Sam could pay Jana's salary under the table.

Except, besides the dishonesty of it, he didn't want her fifty miles away in Sacramento. He wanted her close by, under his nose so he could make sure she was taking care of herself. If she was down in Sac, he'd be worrying about her every day. He had to balance that with the risk of her discovering more about him, and his motive for buying the shop, than he wanted her to learn.

Wariness still tightened her mouth with tension. "Why would you do this, Sam?"

He groped for a response. "You're a friend, Jana. Shouldn't I take care of my friends?"

She laid her hand against her still-flat belly. "I don't have a whole lot of choices. I can't live on the street until July."

"I would never let you do that."

For an instant, he thought he saw the glimmer of tears. Then she glanced out the window, face hidden as she stared into the darkness.

"Fine. I'll take the job." She pushed to her feet. "Jobs. Both of them."

Another knife of anxiety speared through him. "Great."

"Until the baby's born and maybe a little after, if that's okay. In the fall I'll want to start classes at the junior college down in Folsom. I'll probably need to get a job down there."

That she'd be here only until September set off a twang inside him. "You can stay as long as you want."

"Then I'll start cleaning up the apartment tomorrow."

"We can do it together."

Frying pan in one hand and spatula in the other, she elbowed past him on the way to the sink. "Don't you have a deadline or something?"

"I have a month off before I start my next book." When she gave him a fishy look, he raised his hands, palms out. "Gospel truth. You can call my agent and ask him."

Jana shrugged, then started swishing some soapy water in the frying pan. "We'll go over together, then. Get the work done quicker." She tossed him a look over her shoulder. "So I can get out of your way faster."

She rinsed the pan and spatula and set them in the drainer. The bowls they'd used for dinner prep she loaded into the dishwasher. He would have stepped in to do it himself if he wasn't sure she'd bite his head off at the shoulders.

Finished with washing up, she dried her hands on a kitchen towel. "What's with the cake?"

"Birthday cake from last October. Faith made it for me."

"Oh."

"It's been in the freezer ever since. We kept meaning to pull it out and share the rest of it."

"But she got the Rolex and the kiss-off instead."

He squirmed at Jana's near nose-on assessment. "It was a tennis bracelet."

She grinned and tossed the kitchen towel aside. Then her grin faded as worry put shadows under her eyes. "It's the right thing to do, isn't it? Having the baby, giving it up for adoption."

A dozen bromides flitted through his brain. If Jana were a character in one of his stories, he'd have any number of comforting lines to feed her.

But this was real life. He couldn't lie. "I don't know, Jana."

Tears glimmered in her eyes. Without thinking, he pressed his hand against her face. A teardrop escaped, trailing down her cheek as she stared up at him.

That was as far as he should have taken it. Except she took that last step and wrapped her arms around his waist. All the times he'd hugged her, held her, it had felt like friendship. But today, right now, she was a woman in his arms.

That didn't mean he had to let his mind wander along any of those crazy paths temptation suggested. She only needed his comfort, just as she had dozens of times over the years.

But then she looked up at him, eyes wide, lips parting, breath hitching in her throat. A devil perched on his shoulder, calling out instructions, goading him into doing something he damn well shouldn't do. Not when it was Jana in his arms, hurting and confused.

Then her eyes drifted shut. The sight of those delicate lids, the way she'd tipped her face up to his, blew all his good intentions out of the water. All he could think about were her lips and lowering his mouth to hers.

Chapter Four

Holy crap, what was she doing?

Getting all wussy and teary and all but falling into Sam's arms. Yeah, her heart just about felt split in two every time she thought about handing over her baby to someone else, but that didn't give her the right to hang all over Sam, expect him to fix everything for her. She was acting just like her mother used to.

And tipping her head back, closing her eyes—she wasn't asking him to plant a big wet one on her, was she? Even though the world would have tipped end over end on its axis before it crossed Sam's mind to lip-lock with her. Even though getting him to kiss her was exactly what her mother would do. Step one, get a man to make your problems go away. Step two...

Open your eyes, Jana ordered herself. Except now she was terrified to look, afraid of the expression she'd see on Sam's face. Complete bewilderment, most likely. Or even worse, embarrassment.

She pulled out of his arms, escaping the warm circle of his embrace with her eyes still shut. She opened them as she turned on her heel, the move upsetting her fragile equilibrium. Dizziness washed over her, goading her to reach for Sam. No chance she'd tiptoe into that sand trap again. She grabbed for the island instead, gripping cool granite as she slid a sidelong glance toward him.

He was rubbing the side of his face, maybe trying to figure out what the heck had just happened. Worry creased his brow. Her sissy tears had probably put those lines there. With confusion spinning a hamster wheel in her stomach, inexplicable tears still clawing the back of her throat, she stretched her mouth into a smile.

"I'm dead on my feet." She sidled along the island, keeping it between them. "You mind if I give Faith's wonder cake a pass?"

His X-ray stare bored through her. "Are you okay?"

"Great. Just tired." With a sketchy wave, she scooted from the kitchen. He called her name, but she wasn't about to turn around again.

She heard his footsteps behind her but had the door to the guest room shut before he caught up. Nausea, regret and grief braided themselves into an intricate knot inside her as she pushed herself toward the bed. She shucked her jeans and climbed under the covers, reaching up to shut off the bedside lamp before curling into a ball.

She still had to brush her teeth and pee. After her nap, she wasn't really all that sleepy anyway. But she felt torn apart in a million directions, even though she had no right to feel that way. She had a job and a place to stay. The huge weight that had ridden piggyback all the way here from Portland had taken a hike. But there was still all this emotional junk floating around inside of her that made no sense.

It all revolved around Sam and the moment she thought she wanted him to kiss her. It made her cringe inside, not just because he'd think she was still that fourteen-year-old kid with a crush on him, but also because of her mother.

She never wanted to be like her mother, always finagling the men in her life to solve her problems. Then came the payoff—a few days or weeks or sometimes months of mattress wrestling before she sent her savior on his way.

Yuck. Jana had sworn she would never live her life that way. She might be the world's worst screwup—she had to admit she'd inherited that crappy set of genes from her mother—but she wasn't bartering her way out of anything with sex.

Now, scrunched up in bed, she replayed that impulse to kiss Sam. Did she have more in common with her mother than she wanted to admit? Sam gives her what she needs—boom, give the boy a smooch. She could even see the same pattern with Ian. She'd been longing for someone to see her as special, to care about her and only her. Ian put on his show of love, and within days she was tumbling into his bed.

Her skin crawled at the thought, her nausea deepening. She gritted her teeth, bound and determined not to lose the meal she'd just shared with Sam. Gulping in a breath, she managed to get her stomach to settle somewhat.

She didn't care how strong a grip her

mother's genetics had on her DNA. No way, no how was Jana going to mess things up with Sam. He was her all-time best friend in the world. She would die if she stepped over the line, made some stupid pass at him and destroyed their friendship.

Pushing back the covers, she padded into the bathroom to take care of business. She still didn't feel very sleepy, so she dug through the box of books Sam had brought in. She'd read them all more than once, but she could always find something new each time through.

She found the one he'd given her for her twelfth birthday. Angling the book up to the bedside lamp, she turned to the title page. Above his signature he'd inscribed, "Jana, try to stay out of trouble." Advice well worth following.

Settling back against the pillows, she turned to the book's prologue and immediately immersed herself in the story. Just past midnight, when even the riveting story couldn't keep her eyes from drifting shut, she dropped the paperback on the bed and switched off the light. Her dreams were full of Sam—as Trent Garner. It was just like a movie, Sam chasing down bad guys. Except instead of fighting with a gun like Trent would, Sam threw pieces of chocolate cake.

She woke at seven, tired and cranky and more than a little bit sick to her stomach contemplating that chocolate cake. And the French toast she made for her and Sam's breakfast proved to be a bad choice. All that butter and sugary maple syrup didn't sit right. Not to mention Sam barely said a word the whole time they ate.

He continued the silent treatment as they drove into town in his 1946 Hudson pickup, with Jana gulping to keep that breakfast down. It wasn't that he seemed angry or anything. More likely she'd screwed everything up last night with that moment of weakness, and now Sam was probably too embarrassed to talk to her.

Then as he reached the last stop sign before pulling onto Carson Road, he reached across the bench seat, took her hand and squeezed it, his quiet voice matching the stillness of the post-storm mist. "It's all going to work out, Jana."

That just made her want to cry like she had last night, which she was absolutely not going to do. She pressed her lips tightly together, gave him a squeeze back, then tugged free to drop her hand in her lap.

Sam took a side road, pulling in behind the row of businesses that lined the south side of Carson Road. He parked the Hudson behind the third building down, carefully nosing the moss-green classic truck beside a Dumpster.

"Wait," he told her as he opened the door.

He was going to help her out of the cab as if she were some kind of invalid. She felt a smidgen of pleasure at the gesture but mostly irritated that he felt the need. Squelching pleasure, she pushed open her door and jumped out before he got halfway around the back of the truck. She caught his scowl as her feet hit the asphalt pavement.

Shouldering past him to the bed of the truck, she grabbed the caddy of cleaning supplies and tucked a roll of paper towels under her arm. "Can you get the tools? Or do you need a hand?"

She saw the objections dancing in his eyes. He didn't even want her to carry the light-weight caddy, with its couple of bottles of Windex and 409. He wasn't about to let her lift a finger to tote a power tool inside.

"I've got it," he muttered, reaching in the bed for a gigantic toolbox. The way he narrowed his gaze on her, she wondered if he was assessing whether he could tuck her under his arm and carry her in as well, like a roll of paper towels.

She sidled off toward the back door. A set of stairs angled above the door, leading to a second story.

Sam headed for the stairs. "We'll want to start up here."

She followed, waiting a step or two down from the postage stamp–size landing as he opened the door. Behind her, beyond the screen of ponderosa pines, she could hear traffic whipping by on Highway 50 a quarter mile away.

"Like I told you, it's a mess," he said as he set his toolbox inside. He opened the door wider to let her in.

He wasn't kidding. The place looked more like a storage room than living quarters, with boxes piled waist-high along the walls. More boxes and trash littered the kitchen area at one end. The threadbare carpet that led down the hall was a dust bunny habitat.

But with its living room-kitchen combo

maybe ten by fifteen feet in dimension, this part of the apartment wasn't a whole lot smaller than what she'd shared with Ian in Portland. And when she headed down the hall, frightening the dust bunnies into the corners, she saw that the bedroom might even be a little bit bigger.

She checked across the hall and wrinkled her nose. "The bathroom is disgusting."

Sam edged in beside her. "I'll have it gutted. Down to the studs. Replace everything with new."

She squinted up at him. "It just needs a good cleaning." With trepidation she lifted the toilet lid. "Okay, new toilet. But the rest is okay."

Sam got a mulish expression on his face. "I don't want you living in a rattrap."

"And I don't want you spending buckets of money on me." She backed out of the bathroom, again herding dust bunnies down the hallway. "It's bad enough you're giving me this place, this job. I can't let you turn it into a Jana McPartland charity case."

Towering over her in the living room, he shoved his hands into the pockets of his jeans. But as he spoke, he wouldn't quite look at her. "I would have had to fix this place up anyway."

He sounded as if he was trying to convince himself as well as her. As if he wasn't even sure himself why he'd bought this white elephant.

"A complete remodeling would take too much time," she pointed out. "I don't want to have to hang out at your place that long."

He scowled. "This bathroom looks like a toxic waste dump."

"Let me see what I can do with some cleanup. If it's still gross, you can bring in the sledgehammer."

Except she would work her fingers to the bone excavating those layers of dirt before she'd let him empty his bank account on her behalf. Okay, he'd have to plate everything in gold to put a dent in his fortune, but still.

Sam shrugged. "I'll start moving those boxes downstairs. Give us some room. We can go through them later."

He retreated down the hall, shoulders still hunched over. Jana stared after him, wondering what was bugging him. Was he having second thoughts about making the job offer now that he saw what a disaster this place was? Was he considering how to let her down easy, tell her this wasn't going to work after all?

Panic stabbed her, competing with her nausea. She refused to let herself give in to it. She'd just work her buns off here, get the bathroom in tip-top shape so Sam could see it wasn't so bad after all. That she could be trusted to do her part. She couldn't give him a reason to change his mind.

Grabbing the scrub brush and cleanser, she folded herself over the edge of the tub. Wetting the brush and sprinkling it liberally with cleanser, she attacked the worst of the stains.

Sam stacked the last two boxes from the living room on top of one another and elbowed open the door. It had started to drizzle when he had returned from carrying the previous load down. As he carefully made his way downstairs, the raindrops beaded on his face and eyelashes, making it hard to see. Slipping inside the shop's back door, he hoped that whatever was in the top box could stand a little moisture.

He supposed it wouldn't matter if anything was ruined, since he'd be buying new supplies and merchandise anyway. Except he hadn't the first clue what exactly he wanted to fill this boondoggle of a shop with. Christmas stuff. Decorations. Lights. Ornaments. Where he'd find them, how he'd choose them, he had no idea.

That Jana was here to help him through the minefield of his cockeyed notion filled him with both relief and dismay. Relief because he could trust her not to belittle his idea and because given her crazy imagination, she'd get this shop together in no time. Dismay because of the armpit of an apartment he was saddling her with.

He'd done only the most cursory walk-through when he'd closed on this place. Stupid, yes. He'd been scrupulous about every detail when he'd bought his estate. But the dream of what the shop could be had lodged itself inside him, locking rose-colored glasses over his eyes. He hadn't been back since he'd signed the paperwork, had forgotten how nasty the bathroom was.

With the last set of boxes dumped in the middle of the cluttered shop, Sam locked up and returned upstairs. He should have just insisted on bringing in a crew to rehab that entire bathroom. He didn't like the thought of pregnant Jana living in squalor.

But when he poked his head inside the bathroom, he was surprised to see that the tub just about sparkled it was so clean. Looking up at him over her shoulder, Jana smiled, the pride in her work shining in her face. His heart kicked in his chest, and he was swamped by the urge to sit beside her and gather her in his arms.

Pushing on the edge of the tub, she folded her feet under her to rise. He reached for her arm and helped her up. But he let her go right away, not liking the ache in his chest.

She gestured at the tub. "Told you it would come clean. The toilet's a loss and the floor is curling up in the corners, so those definitely need replacing. But I think I can get the stains out of the sink and a little paint should fix up the vanity."

"Let me take a look at that floor." They danced in the small space, him edging in toward the far wall, her taking his place in the doorway. He pressed with his toe where the old linoleum curled up. "Dry rot." He showed her how it gave under his foot. "I'll have to call someone to fix it."

"You told me you worked construction all through college. Why can't you do it yourself?"

Out of long-forgotten habit, his mind went through the steps needed to repair dry rot. He shook his head. "Why should I when I can pay someone?"

She made a face at him. "You've gotten so used to throwing money at a problem. Are you afraid of a little hard work?"

"Of course not." He remembered dragging deadfall from the creek yesterday morning, how good the physical labor had felt. "You said yourself you wanted this place finished as quickly as possible."

"I do." With a sigh, she leaned against the doorjamb. "But I don't want you spending tons of money. Plus, this is your shop—don't you want to be the one who fixes it up?"

Did he? He hadn't really thought that far ahead. He'd gone completely on impulse when he'd bought the shop, with a fuzzy, distant dream of Christmas leading him by the nose. Now that he was here, with Jana's arrival and her and her baby's needs factoring into the picture, he was going to have to start fleshing out his amorphous fantasies, pronto.

"It makes sense I should do some of it," he agreed. The feeling of gratification that welled inside surprised him. It wasn't as if he avoided hard work—constructing a thriller novel took a hell of a lot of brain power. But he felt a sense of renewal throwing himself into this project.

"I'll still have to hire out some of the work," he told her. He wasn't going to touch the electrical work and he hated plumbing.

"Give me another half hour or so to finish

the sink. Then we'll go through and get all the tasks organized and prioritized."

"Watch the floor in that corner," he warned her. He put his full weight on it. Soft, but it wouldn't give way. He felt a chill at the thought of her falling through.

She sidled back into the bathroom, carrying her cleanser and scrub brush to the sink. "I'm glad we're doing it ourselves. It'll seem more like a home then."

He looked around at the ratty bathroom, then down at the shredded carpet that lined the hall. His chest tightened a third time, and he started wondering about heart problems. It amazed him that this meant so much to her, that she seemed so happy in this ragged-around-the-edges studio when she could have been living in his much nicer guest room.

He knew Jana had grown up with as little as he had. But where he'd enjoyed increasing wealth over the past decade, she'd struggled from the moment she'd turned eighteen when her mother tossed her out. To appreciate so little, to see this apartment's potential as a home, just emphasized the difficult place she'd found herself in when Ian walked out on her.

Stepping across the hall to the bedroom, Sam left her to her work. There were more boxes stored in here, several more loads to transfer downstairs. As he lifted the first two and started down the hall, he heard Jana belting out "The Star-Spangled Banner," flat and off-key. She never could sing a note, but, damn, did she sound happy.

Chapter Five

By the end of the day, the sink and tub were clean, the vanity sanded and ready for paint, the dry rot in the floor repaired and the toilet removed. They'd taken stock of the kitchen—cart away the refrigerator, oven okay, but the dishwasher smelled like a petri dish culture. Sam had an extra microwave at the house that Jana could take—he would have bought her a new one, but she talked him down from that position. There wasn't a stick of furniture in the entire place, so that required a shopping spree.

With a trip agreed to for the next day while the contractors were in working on carpet and such, Jana made her way, zombielike, through take-out pizza back at Sam's, then all but fell into bed in exhaustion. She seemed to spend the night in constant motion in her dreams, waking in the morning feeling more sapped of energy than when she'd gone to bed.

When she stumbled into the kitchen and discovered Sam at the stove flipping pancakes, a pile of misshapen flapjacks behind him on the island, she nearly burst into tears. She had to turn away before he saw her, step back into the great room so she could pull herself together. She couldn't quite reason why she wanted to sob, but it had something to do with being pregnant, wiped out and completely overwhelmed by Sam making pancakes for her for breakfast.

She hated pancakes. A fact she'd never had the opportunity to mention to Sam. Unlike

French toast, pancakes got all soggy and gummy when you poured syrup on them. Her stomach was already doing its usual gymnastic floor routine of backflips and somersaults. Now she'd have to drop pancakes into the mix. Because no way, no how could she refuse what Sam had made for her.

Swallowing back tears and nausea, Jana re-entered the kitchen. This time, Sam grinned at her over his shoulder. She felt so darn lucky to have a buddy as great as Sam and couldn't help but smile in return. Then as their gazes locked and Sam's smile reshaped into something softer, sexier, her heart thumped heavily in her chest. Suddenly, it was a little hard to breathe.

She tore her gaze away, shifting it to the sagging stack of pancakes, grateful when the nausea returned. She had no intention of going down that same path she'd tripped down the night before last. She couldn't risk the friendship she so desperately wanted to keep intact.

Grabbing an overripe banana from the bowl on the island, she stripped off the peel and chomped a bite of the fruit. "So, you can make pancakes at least," she said over a mouthful of banana.

"From a mix." He gestured at the box lying on its side next to the cooktop.

Jana picked up the box. "You used it all?" she asked, feeling its featherweight.

"A lot of trial and error my first time out." He pressed a toe on the pedal for the trash can, showed her the burnt pancakes lining the bottom. "Mostly error."

She got out the syrup and the eggs, figuring the more she filled her stomach with other stuff, the fewer pancakes she'd have to eat. By the time they sat down in the breakfast nook, she'd already wolfed down two scrambled eggs straight from the skillet. The two pancakes she ate didn't seem to settle as badly on a mostly full stomach, especially since she dipped each bite in the puddle of syrup on her plate rather than pouring the stuff on top.

Sam inhaled the last of his stack of six, then leaned back in his chair, fingers locked on his belly. "I was thinking…"

Her radar shot up. "What?"

She saw the wary look in his eyes. "While we're out, I wanted to pick you up a few things."

She pushed her plate aside, not liking the direction he was going. "Such as?"

"Stuff for the apartment, of course. Linens, towels, shower curtain, miniblinds."

"We already talked about all that last night." She could accept those purchases because she'd be leaving them all behind after the baby was born and she moved out.

"I also thought you'd need some other odds and ends." Now his gaze drifted out the window where the sun fought for supremacy with scattered clouds. "Clothes. Shoes."

She squashed her irritation. "Why do you keep wanting to buy me stuff?"

"You need clothes, Jana. I didn't have to go through that duffel to know you don't have more than a couple of changes. And you're going to need more than T-shirts once you get..." He flapped his hands out in front of himself.

He was right, she didn't have nearly enough to get her through her pregnancy. Two pair of maternity jeans and a few large T-shirts. "Take me to the thrift store, then. I can find some stuff there."

He shook his head. "I want to buy you new."

"Why spend all that money when hand-me-downs work just as well?"

"Because it's all I know how to do!" He shoved back his chair, jumping to his feet. "It's the only way I know how to help you. I can't cook worth a damn. I can't transform Ian into the world's best father. I can't answer even one of the questions I know you've got racing around in your head."

He picked up his plate and all but tossed it on the counter beside the sink. "But I have money, and spending it is something I know how to do. Just let me spread a little of that wealth on you."

She carefully considered her response, not wanting to offend him. "I appreciate it, Sam. Really I do. I just don't know why you'd want to."

"We're friends."

"I'm glad you think so." Even more than she was willing to admit to him. "But I feel a little like…" She considered how to say what had been eating at her. Then just blurted it out. "I can't give back to you the way you're giving to me. And don't you say a word about how I'm working for you. You know everything you're offering me is way above and beyond."

He leaned against the center island, arms crossed. "You don't have to give me anything in return. All these years I've known you, since you were a kid… You have to know you're like a sister to me. Family."

That took the wind out of her sails. It sure made it crystal clear that she didn't have to worry about the sex thing with him, even if she'd wanted to follow in her mother's footsteps. She ought to be relieved. She was, really. It was perfect, wasn't it, for him to think of her as a sister?

For Sam to consider her family…a cartoon heart took off from her chest. She'd never known her father, had been an afterthought to her mother. The only family she'd had all those years growing up was what she'd found at Estelle's. She'd always hoped she meant more to Sam that just some twerpy kid always clinging to his coattails.

"Okay, big brother." She got to her feet and

walked over to him. "If blowing a few bucks on your little sister makes you happy, go for it. As long as you don't go overboard."

He smiled again, that same drop-dead gorgeous grin that probably sold more books than the actual stories he wrote. No wonder they plastered his face on the back dust jacket.

He threw his arms around her and tugged her close. She reluctantly wrapped her own arms around his waist in turn. Just because it felt so good rubbing her palms against the back of his thick wool sweater didn't mean there was anything to their hug other than brotherly-sisterly affection.

Except that her imagination was marching out suggestions that didn't feel the least bit sisterly. She swatted them aside, resisted the urge to snuggle even closer to Sam, to press her mouth against his chest and kiss him.

She might never have had a brother, but she

was darn sure that wasn't something she might have done with one.

She took a big step back. "You made breakfast. I'll clean up." Her hands, looking for an excuse to touch him again, got busy filling the sink with hot soapy water.

She could feel him behind her, still rooted to the same spot. When she sneaked a peek, he was staring at her.

A tremor shivered up her spine. "What?"

He seemed to shake himself, then took the long way around the island. "I'll get the car."

"I'll meet you outside in just a sec," she called out. "Okay?"

No answer from Sam. He just skittered out of the kitchen and toward the garage.

Had she done it again? Somehow let slip her thoughts through her actions? Was he able to decipher her fantasies from the way she'd rubbed his back?

She squeezed her eyes shut, trying to

remember just how she'd touched him. It had seemed innocent, but who knows how Sam might have interpreted it?

She'd have to stop touching him altogether. She couldn't trust herself not to do it wrong. If she screwed things up with Sam like she'd messed up so much else in her life, it would break her heart.

So from now on, it was hands off. No excuses.

Sam backed his 1960 Edsel Villager Wagon from its slot in the garage, taking care not to nick the car's finish on the side of the garage door. Considering where his mind was—certainly not on the pristine turquoise-and-white paint job of his cherished nine-passenger Edsel—he wasn't sure he should be behind the wheel at all.

It had been an innocent gesture, taking Jana in his arms for a hug. What he'd said about thinking of her as family, as a sister, had been gospel truth. He'd never fully articulated that to himself before that moment, but as soon as he spoke it out loud, realization had shot up like a flame.

Then he drew her in his arms and felt her softness pressed against his chest. And started going way off course. Contemplating kisses along her brow. Exploring that shadow behind her ear. The tenderness of her slender throat.

Sam slammed on the brakes, a bare inch from ramming the back of the Villager into a cypress tree. He pounded the heel of his hand into his forehead a few times, wishing he could reset his brain the same way he did with his computer's power button. But he'd let those thoughts in, and now he'd have to deal with them. Box them in a corner, throw a heavy blanket over the box and a boulder on top of the blanket. Maybe the Empire State Building atop the boulder.

As he pulled up in front of the house to wait for Jana, another worry squirmed inside his stomach. Just because he considered her family, that didn't give him any guarantees. She could still walk out the door like his mother had, disappear from his life as his sister, Madelena, had. Betray him the way Aunt Barbara had when she'd drop-kicked him into foster care.

Except Jana wouldn't…would she? Leave him, disappear, betray him. Of course not. She was different than that. He could count on her.

Yeah, she'd experienced that momentary insanity and gone off with Ian. But she'd realized her mistake, had come to her senses. And it was him she'd come to when she knew she needed help. Not Tony or Rebecca. Not even Estelle. She came to him. That meant something.

He'd be okay as long as he kept his head on straight. As long as he didn't start thinking about her like he had about Faith. Or Shawna or Cyndy or Patricia. Or any of the other women who had drifted in, then out of his life.

The front door opened and Jana stepped out, locking up with his house key. This was far too much heavy thought for so early in the morning. He was making this thing way more complicated than he needed to. Too used to dreaming up complex plotlines for his thrillers, he sometimes let that tendency creep into the real world. He'd overthink things.

He and Jana were friends. Close as family. Nothing more to it.

Then she climbed into the car, her smile so radiant he felt its effects clear to his toes. Without a word, she sent him into another maelstrom of confusion.

Before Jana could again throw out the suggestion that they make their purchases at the local thrift store, Sam made a big deal out of insisting they buy furniture at a high-end

designer home store in Sacramento. As pre-
dicted, Jana went ballistic and demanded he
take her to the local big-box discount place
instead. Satisfied that he'd gotten her off the
thrift store bandwagon, he crossed his fingers
that she wouldn't figure out she'd been
snookered until the Villager was safely parked.

They pushed separate carts, which also got
an argument out of Jana. Even after Sam pa-
tiently explained that the stuff they were
picking up was bulky and would require two
carts—for example, for the bedding and
window coverings—she still kept up the
scowl. That sunny smile she'd greeted him
with when she'd first climbed into the wagon
had vanished.

Her mood darkened as they proceeded
through the store, as he made arrangements to
have the futon sofa and easy chair delivered
tomorrow, as he pulled out his credit cart to
check out. She turned so pale when she saw

the total that he would have taken her arm to support her if she hadn't already had such a death grip on the counter.

When they finally pushed the towering pile of purchases out to the parking lot, Sam waited until they'd unloaded and Jana had a chance to climb in the car and get her seat belt on. Then he turned toward her, cocking one leg up on the bench seat.

"You want to explain the Dr. Jekyll and Ms. Hyde bit this morning?"

To her credit, she gave him a straight answer. "You're doing too much for me. You even got me a cell phone, for heaven's sake."

"It's just a few extra bucks on my current cell plan. Besides, I thought we agreed on this." He gestured at the packed rear seats.

"We did. But the reality of it..." She locked her fingers together. "Up until now, the only things you've given me were copies of your books."

"I took you out to McDonald's a few times."

"When I was eleven." She huffed an impatient breath. "Don't minimize this, Sam. You just dropped a lot of bucks on me and plan to spend more. Stuff for the apartment, maternity clothes. And so far I haven't done a darn thing to earn any of it."

"Why do you feel you have to earn it? Why can't I just give it to you?"

"Because…" She opened her mouth as she seemed to grope for an explanation. Then her gaze skittered away from him, out the Villager's broad windshield. When she looked at him, a beguiling wash of pink colored her cheeks.

Jana's lips were still parted, moist from where her tongue had wet them. The chilly interior of the wagon spiked with heat, as if their bodies were warming it. Her soft brown eyes widened as she stared up at him. Sam's good intentions threatened to take a powder, and he was nine-tenths of a second from reaching for her.

At the last instant, he wrapped his fingers around the steering wheel, focusing out the windshield instead of on her. "I never gave you stuff before because you didn't need it. You need it now. You've got to have sheets to sleep on and a blanket to keep you warm. You'll need to wear something for the next seven months."

She sighed. "When it's over, I can just leave the stuff with you, okay? Maybe donate the clothes to the thrift store?"

"Sure. That makes sense." She wasn't likely to need those voluminous shirts and stretchy jeans again any time soon. But a part of him wanted her to keep what he'd given her. Even that silly little Eeyore bedside lamp they'd found in the children's section.

Which confused the hell out of him. He couldn't care less if Faith had thrown that outrageously expensive tennis bracelet into the Sacramento River after she'd left his house.

But he wished Jana would want to keep a cheapo Eeyore lamp.

Well, he'd known Jana longer. She meant more to him. As a friend, of course. As a close-as-family, almost-like-a-sister friend.

Tucking away his confusion, Sam headed back out to Highway 50. Last night on the Internet, he'd scoped out the best price for a dishwasher and fridge and found a place in Folsom, twenty miles west. The appliances he chose wouldn't be the cheapest, which he refused to buy no matter how much Jana squawked, nor the most expensive, which should keep her complaints to a minimum.

Once they got to the store, she ended up wandering off to the music aisle, leaving him to deal with the oversolicitous salesman. Jana met up with him again just as they finished writing up the sale, two CDs in her hand.

"I want to pay for these," she told him, "so take them out of my first check."

The twentysomething salesclerk, tall and skinny with a smudge of hair on his chin, gave Jana the once-over with a grin. "So you two are together?"

Jana didn't show even an iota of interest in the eager young man, but annoyance boiled up inside Sam nevertheless. He wanted to hustle Jana out of there, away from the salesclerk's avid gaze. A guy didn't want another guy looking at his sister like that, right?

Before he could tug Jana toward the exit, remind her they had one more stop to make for a bed, a woman's voice called out to him. "Sam?"

He turned to see Faith at the other end of the aisle of dishwashers. Behind her, a short, stocky man with thinning hair was studying a microwave.

She murmured to her companion, then approached Sam with a tentative smile. The man followed. Jana had shaken off the salesclerk and eyed Faith with curiosity.

"This is Ed," Faith said.

A light of recognition flickered on. "From your law office," Sam said, shaking the man's hand.

"On the real estate side," Ed said with a proprietary touch to Faith's shoulder.

Not just coworkers, then. Barely more than a week since he'd ended things with Faith and here she was with Ed. Now the resignation in her face that day made more sense. He supposed he couldn't blame her, considering his benign neglect at the end of their relationship.

Except he ought to feel something more than indifference, shouldn't he? He nudged Jana forward. "You remember me mentioning Jana McPartland."

Smiles and handshakes all around, then Faith gave Ed's arm a squeeze. "Excuse me a minute, sweetheart. Can I talk to you, Sam?"

Jana's gaze narrowed on his ex-girlfriend as Faith walked with him out of earshot. He wouldn't put it past Jana to put on some kind of superradar so she could follow the conversation.

With a side-by-side refrigerator obstructing their view of the others, Faith took her stand. "I want you to know Ed was a perfect gentleman those last few months before you kissed me off. He let me cry on his shoulder, never made one wrong move."

"It's okay. I understand."

Her face hardened. "Don't think it didn't hurt, even knowing what I was getting into with you."

Well-placed sucker punch, he thought. But who could blame her? "I'm sorry, Faith. I never meant to—"

"I gave that damn bracelet away. Donated it to Goodwill."

He almost laughed but kept the impulse down with an effort. He couldn't wait to share the joke with Jana. Leaning back to get a clear line of sight between refrigerators, he managed to make eye contact with her. She looked about ready to die from the tediousness of making conversation with Ed.

Despite his inattention, Faith kept talking. "At least now you've got what you always wanted."

His head whipped back around to her. "What?"

"Jana. As much as you waxed euphoric over her while we were dating, Jana this and Jana that, I'm glad the two of you are finally together."

"We're not together." Anxiety at the thought marched through his stomach. "She's an old friend. And just a kid."

Faith gave him a long considering look. "Okay."

He felt the need to clarify. "She showed up a couple days ago. I'm just helping her out."

Another long look, then she patted his

arm. "I have to get back. Ed and I are on lunch hour."

They all parted company, then Sam paid for Jana's bargain bin CDs—a loan, she insisted again—and they returned to the car. He told her how Faith had donated the tennis bracelet to Goodwill, expecting her to laugh at his expense. But Jana was quiet as they continued west on Highway 50 toward the mattress store, her expression thoughtful.

They'd just pulled into the parking lot when she delivered a finish to the one-two punch Faith had started. "You buy women things because it's safer."

"I don't know what you mean," he said, although he suspected that was a lie.

She turned to him as he nosed the car into a slot. "It's safer than giving them more of yourself."

"Maybe buying them things is my way of giving myself."

She stared at him, and he could see her working out that possibility in her mind. Then she shook her head. "I don't think so."

He wanted to tell her she was wrong, that she didn't know a damn thing about him. Except wouldn't that prove her point, that even after all these years she didn't really know him, because he gave her so little of himself?

Better to just ignore what she'd said, pretend it didn't apply to him. So he held his tongue as he and Jana climbed out of the car, headed for the store. As he prepared himself to buy his way out of an honest look at himself once again.

Chapter Six

Jana felt a little better figuring out what she had about Sam. She was still worried about all that money she had no way of repaying. But in a strange way, she guessed he was getting something out of his generosity. Protection against anyone—in this case, Jana—digging any deeper.

She would have preferred it if he'd trusted her enough not to need that kind of distraction. But in a way it provided her protection, too. Because he was buying her stuff to make him feel better and certainly not—insert laugh track here—because he was hot for her bod.

In any case, she let him choose the double bed, didn't even look at the price. She tried it out because he insisted, although that was pretty awkward, lying on the bare mattress with Sam and the saleswoman standing over her. The chic-to-the-max saleswoman recognized Sam and was gushing all over him, telling him she'd read everything he'd written. Sam seemed to forget Jana was there as he scrawled his autograph on a piece of printer paper and turned on that million-watt smile for the woman.

Not that Jana was jealous, any more than she'd been when she'd seen the gorgeous Faith in the appliance store. She knew what kind of women Sam went for, and they weren't tomboyish and boobless with mousy brown hair. Like her.

Of course, Sam talked the saleswoman into arranging delivery for tomorrow, just as he had all the other stuff. Paid extra for it, too. Which was great—all the sooner for her to get out of Sam's place and into the apartment.

Sam had cheered up by the time they got back into the car. He was smiling as he carefully pulled the Villager out of its space.

"Did you ask her out?" Jana asked, even though she really didn't want to know.

"Who?" He had his eyes on the road as he merged the vehicle onto the freeway.

"The saleswoman. Ms. I'm-your-biggest-fan."

Now he glanced over at her. "Why would I do that?"

"Did you?"

He actually blushed. "She gave me her number."

Jana laughed even though she felt hollow inside. "Of course she did."

He scowled. "I didn't ask for it."

She forced herself to laugh again. "You know, as your assistant, I could buy the parting gifts early. That way when you're ready to call it quits, you're all prepared."

She knew the instant the words were out of her mouth that they would hurt him. It was like something her teenage self would have said, the unthinking screwup she'd always been. Apparently still was.

She saw how tightly his hands gripped the steering wheel, the way his jaw worked with tension. "I'm sorry. That was stupid. It's hormones or tiredness or just that I'm a complete idiot."

He was quiet as they passed Folsom, then continued past the foothill towns west of Placerville. "You have a point," he said finally. "My track record sucks."

She let out a long breath of air, grateful he wasn't totally mad at her, that he wasn't about to pull over and boot her out of the wagon. She cautiously suggested, "Maybe you should give the whole girl thing a rest for a while."

He pulled off the freeway at the Golden Arches, glanced over at her at the red light and stared at her for a long time, until the guy behind him honked at the green. "Maybe so," he said quietly as he pulled through.

There was a message in those blue, blue eyes, one she couldn't decipher. But it sent a finger of sensation up her spine and started her imagination all over again thinking of possibilities.

After lunch, Sam could see Jana was beat. He drove her straight up to the house rather than stopping at the apartment as he'd originally intended. They could always drop off their purchases tomorrow. The contractors finishing off carpet and vinyl installation in the apartment were probably still working anyway. He and Jana would just get in their way.

While Jana napped, Sam holed up in his office. The wind had picked up, gusts sending puffy white clouds scudding across the deep blue sky. The oaks and pines visible through his office window moved in a free-form dance as the breeze punched through them.

What Jana had told him earlier about how he bought women stuff to keep them from getting close was still sifting through his mind. It wasn't anything he hadn't realized himself, deep down. He just had never chosen to acknowledge it.

Why shouldn't he keep some of the crap inside to himself? He'd gone through some pretty heavy-duty mojo during his childhood. Did he have to be all touchy-feely and lay that mess on everyone he met? Jana ought to be grateful he hadn't burdened her with his personal nightmare. She knew his mom had walked out on his sister and him—did she have to hear the gory details of the whole ter-rifying experience?

So it made him feel good to buy stuff for people, to spend his hard-earned money on them. That didn't mean he was substituting money for truth. He didn't owe the truth to everyone in the world. Considering how things had ended up with Faith, it was just as well he'd kept some things to himself.

What about Jana?

Over the years, she'd laid out a lot about her own life, how her mom was such a flake. How her mom was always getting herself into fixes that other people would have to pull her out of. And how her mom had been leaving her alone all hours of the day and night since Jana was eight. Sam hadn't needed that confidence from Jana to know she was a lost soul and a lot like him.

So why not confess some of his old garbage to Jana? She wouldn't go blabbing it to, say, Tony and Rebecca. He could trust her to keep his secrets just as he had his foster mom,

Estelle, although even she didn't know every last detail.

But why tell anyone? That was ancient history. It wasn't as if it had anything to do with who he was today.

Turning back to his computer, he opened up a document filled with notes for his next book. He hadn't planned to start working in earnest until March, but when ideas popped up, he felt compelled to type them in so he wouldn't forget. These past couple days spent with Jana had sparked an inspiration, and he wanted to see where it would take him.

Trent Garner had been a lone wolf for eight years and ten books, loving 'em and leaving 'em by the end of each action-packed story. For the most part, women had always been window dressing in the complex plots. There was a female police chief in the jurisdiction where the fictional P.I. lived, as well as a female judge who drifted in and out of the novels, but they were both older women and more sounding boards than actual intimates.

But a new character was trying to insinuate herself into his consciousness. A smart-mouthed female journalist, sharp as a tack, always trying to weasel her way into Trent's business. She wasn't drop-dead gorgeous like the arm candy Trent liked to keep company with. But she was cute and appealing, a fresh-faced twenty-five-year-old to act as a foil to Trent's world-weary midthirties.

By the time he came up for air, it was nearly four o'clock and he could hear Jana moving around in the kitchen. Saving the file and exiting his word processor, he padded downstairs and across the living room. He stopped just out of sight of Jana in the kitchen. She'd changed into the red-and-purple-striped sweater he'd bought her today and had tied one of Mrs. Prentiss's aprons around her waist.

As she chopped onions at the island, she did

a clumsy two-step, her voice a dissonant accompaniment to Don Henley's on Sam's vintage Eagles CD. She never could sing worth a damn. He made a mental note to add that trait to the character description of his new Trent Garner sidekick.

He waited until she'd pressed the hold button on her off-key singing and dropped the onions into the sizzling frying pan. Then he strode into the kitchen. "Hey, what's cooking?"

Tossing the last few diced onions into the pan, she gave him a wary look. "Chili. I found some ground beef in the freezer and thought I'd make some."

"I love chili." Which she knew. That much he'd told her.

She gave the onions a stir, then glanced at him sidelong. "Are we okay?"

"Sure. We're fine." He fussed over the selections in the fruit bowl, finally settling on a golden delicious apple. He wasn't hungry, didn't want it, but had to do something with his hands.

"I'm sorry about the bad joke. That was mean of me."

"Hey, it was funny. Right on the mark." Except it had cut deep. He took a savage bite of the apple. "Anything I can do to help?" he asked around a mouthful.

"Open those cans," she said, pointing with the wooden spoon at a lineup on the center island of chili beans, tomatoes and tomato sauce.

Setting aside the apple, he dutifully carried the cans over to the opener, near the sink. Over the whine of the motor, he brought up the touchy subject that had crossed his mind while he was working upstairs.

"You know you're going to have to contact Ian sooner or later. Get his permission for the adoption."

With her back to him, he couldn't see her face, but her shoulders stiffened. "I know."

He tiptoed a little closer to the minefield. "I could call Darius, my private investigator friend. Tracking missing persons is one of his specialties."

"Not yet."

"Jana—"

"Not yet, please." She faced him. "I know it's something I have to take care of. I'm just not ready."

He got it, then. Contacting Ian, having him sign off on parental rights, would take her one step closer to finalizing her decision to put her baby up for adoption.

Another thought dropped an anchor in his stomach. "Are you hoping he'll come back?" he asked. "That the two of you will get back together?"

Her lip curled in disgust. "Yuck. Absolutely not. I might have been stupid to have hooked up with that loser in the first place, but I'm not completely brainless." She snatched up the cans he'd opened and dumped the contents into a massive pot.

Relief eased the knot in his belly. He'd hated it when she'd disappeared with Ian last year. Not knowing where she was, if she was okay. That sister-brother thing again. It was the same way he used to worry about his sister, Madelena, when she was living with Aunt Barbara and he was in foster care.

Second time in one day he'd thought of Maddie. It had been, what? A decade at least since that phone call from her, one night while Aunt Barbara was out of town. And that had been brief. She'd been a giggly seventeen-year-old, giddy over the fact she'd tracked down the phone number for her forbidden elder brother.

Then five or six years ago, she'd tried again, this time through his agent, since his number was unlisted by then. But he'd been an arrogant horse's ass, recently stung by a girlfriend only interested in his money and a piece of his fame. He'd sent a message back through his agent, refusing Maddie's overture.

Nothing since then. Which probably meant she'd given up on him. She was an adult now, no longer under Aunt Barbara's thumb. She could track him down by e-mail through his Web site, but she hadn't bothered. Or maybe she figured the ball was in his court.

So why hadn't he contacted her? He'd like to think it was because his life was too busy and he just hadn't gotten around to it. But in his heart of hearts, he knew the truth—that he still harbored that stone of resentment inside that he went to foster care but Maddie didn't.

Jana was waving a chili-coated spoon in his face. "Earth to Sam."

He shook off thoughts of his sister. "How long before the chili's ready?"

She eyed him speculatively. "Couple hours at least. I want to make cornbread, too."

"Enough time to play some cards, then."

She set aside the spoon, apparently willing to go along with his change of subject. "Cribbage? Russian rummy?"

"Cribbage first. We'll see where we go from there."

As she untied the apron, slipped it from her body, his mind took off in an entirely unexpected direction. Before he could stop himself, he was picturing Jana taking off her clothes, piece by piece, as they played strip poker.

Lagging behind her so she couldn't see, he slapped himself in the head a couple times to knock some sense in. He'd been doing well the whole day, keeping his distance, avoiding touching her even in the close confines of the car. He'd even kept a strict muzzle on his imagination while she was trying out beds at the mattress store, focusing instead on the endless nattering of the salesclerk so he wouldn't get dragged along by his adolescent libido.

Cribbage. We're playing cribbage, he reminded himself as he tracked down the board and a deck of cards from the sideboard in the living room. But when she settled opposite him on the sofa, feet curled up under her, the sleeves of her sweater pushed up to her elbows, all he could think about was how it would feel to run his finger slowly from the inside of her wrist to the crook of her arm.

Sam didn't have a prayer of winning. Not with his mind handicapped by misplaced lust and Jana playing her usual cutthroat game. It didn't take her long to peg to a win, double-skunking him as winter darkness settled outside and the delectable aroma of chili filled the house.

When they checked out the apartment the next morning, Jana could see the contractors had made a ton of progress. They hadn't finished repairing the kitchen cabinets, and a couple of light fixtures were down to correct code violations, but the new carpet and the flooring in the kitchen and bathroom looked great. It was actually starting to look like a home.

Jana had wanted to repaint the bathroom vanity herself, but Sam nixed that idea. He had a point, though—breathing in paint fumes in that small space wouldn't be good for the baby. So, while Sam gave the contractors a hand in finishing up the final repairs, Jana went downstairs to inventory what was in the boxes.

Before she even started with that chore, she gave the shop a thorough going-over, a pad and pen handy to make notes. The main space, about twenty by twenty, looked as if the previous owner had packed away the merchandise but left everything else right where it stood. The empty shelves were thick with dust, the walls full of holes, big and small, with outlines visible where pictures had hung. The wood floor was stained and in need of refinishing. One of the front windows was cracked and would have to be replaced. Two of the fluorescents in the fixtures above were out.

Listing all the needed repairs on her pad, she moved on to the restroom and office/storeroom situated on either side of the back door. The bathroom was in good shape, but there were a dozen more boxes tucked away in the storeroom that she'd have to go through. The cardboard in the corner of one had been chewed through. She shivered. Rats. The actual, literal kind. She made a note, then returned to the store to start opening boxes.

The slam of the back door at lunchtime announced Sam's arrival. "How's it going?"

"Great. Just finishing the last box."

She turned to smile at him and felt as if the breath had been knocked out of her. Good grief, the man looked good in jeans and a T-shirt—even with his hair a little sweaty from hard work, flecks of white paint dotting his arms and face.

A couple small specks of paint had landed on his forehead. Before she could think better of it, she reached up to rub them away, fingers itching as they drew closer. "You've got some paint—"

He grabbed her wrist, stopping her cold. "I've got it. Thanks." He slipped into the bathroom.

She wanted to kick herself and would have if she didn't have the baby to consider. She'd done great all of yesterday, keeping her hands off him even when she'd won her third game of cribbage and longed to give him a celebratory hug. She couldn't mess that up now.

He returned, face a little damp from washing. "Did you figure out what's what?"

She turned her focus on her morning's work. "I've got everything sorted out into five categories." She pointed as she ticked off what she'd found. "Supplies, like TP for the restroom, register tape, pens, pencils, that sort of thing. Generic merchandise we might be able to use in the store—scented candles, pot-pourri, silk flowers. Over there's stuff we don't need but is worth selling on the Internet for a few bucks."

"We can give the proceeds to Tony's program."

"Sure. I'll need a computer to set up an account at one of the auction sites and a digital camera."

"I've got an older laptop and camera I don't use anymore. What else?" he asked.

"In those boxes—" she pointed "—are a fair number of smaller odds and ends that might not be worth selling but are still good enough to donate to the thrift store. Those boxes over there are Dumpster fodder."

"You're amazing. Great work."

His words set off a glow inside her. That urge to give him a thank-you hug for the compliment bubbled up inside, but she ignored it.

Instead, she showed him her pad. "You

might want to go through and double-check this. I may have missed something."

He scanned the list, then glanced up at her. "You think I'm crazy buying this run-down store? My wacky idea about turning it into a Christmas shop?"

She sensed he was asking more than the surface question and didn't want to say the wrong thing. "I never knew Christmas was such a big deal for you."

He looked away, out the front window at the traffic passing by on Carson Road. "Why wouldn't it be?"

"You never came to the Christmas parties Estelle gave for the kids. I mean, you'd send all kinds of presents, but you'd never be there."

The pad of paper bent under his tight grip. "You know I'm busy."

She should leave it alone. Sam had drawn a line in the sand enough times for her to know that she'd get nowhere trying to cross it. But if this shop was so important to him, shouldn't she know why? Wouldn't that make it easier for her to help him make it a success?

She gulped in a breath. "Except Estelle told me that even when you were a kid living with her, you never liked Christmas. All the other kids would exchange presents, and you'd be sitting in your room, alone."

He whipped around on his heel so fast that Jana took an involuntary step back. "That's none of your business."

His anger tore into her. He'd been irritated with her enough times, impatient, but never enraged like this. He was shaking he was so mad.

Jana hugged herself. "I'm sorry."

Just like that his anger washed away. "Oh, God, I'm sorry, Jana." He crossed the room and wrapped his arms around her. "That was inexcusable."

It took about three seconds for Sam to

soothe her; every moment after that was pure elation. Not good if she was going to keep her head on straight. She pulled back, giving his arm a pat before she stepped clear.

"You're totally forgiven if you'll feed me. I forgot my crackers and my stomach's a little dicey."

"One of the guys went for sandwiches." Unease still cut a line in his brow. "Are you sure you're okay?"

More than okay with him so close, staring down at her. "I'm fine. Except for the ready-to-upchuck part."

He scrubbed a hand through his already messed-up hair. "The whole Christmas thing is kind of complicated for me."

She thought he might tell her more, but then the younger of the two contractors knocked at the back door and stepped inside. He held a bag out to Sam. "There's a couple of sodas on the bottom." He headed back out again.

Sam arranged a couple of boxes sturdy enough to sit on beside a third they could use as a table. Jana wolfed down half her turkey and provolone sub with barely a pause, then took a break to make sure everything settled okay.

"I had a thought last night while I was falling asleep," she said as she sipped her orange soda. "Kind of a variation on your idea for the store."

He split open a bag of chips and laid it out for them to share. "Tell me."

"I do think a Christmas store is cool. But to give it a better chance, what if we made the shop more of an all-around holiday place?"

He munched a potato chip, then took a swallow of cola. "How so?"

"There are always holidays to celebrate. Valentine's Day, Easter, Independence Day. We could stock decorations and other merchandise for holidays year-round. And besides the biggies like Thanksgiving and Christmas, there are all these wacko days like Hug Your Cat Day and Rocky Road Day."

He laughed. "You're making this up."

"Looked it up on the Internet this morning, on your office computer. Before you were up. I hope that was okay."

"Sure. No problem." He looked distracted, as if he was considering her suggestion.

She crossed her fingers. She wasn't exactly known for coming up with fabulous ideas. Sam was too nice to tell her it was stupid, but he might not be able to hide that look in his eyes if the thought crossed his mind.

But his grin told her his opinion even before he spoke. "You are brilliant."

She just about swooned at the second compliment from Sam in less than an hour. Not that he was stingy with them; in fact, he'd always been her biggest booster. But after so many recent stumbles in her life, hearing Sam's praise was overwhelming.

"So we'd rotate the stock depending on the season?" he asked. "We'd have to get creative to come up with the right merchandise for some of your wacky days—"

"Like stuffed cats and bags of chocolate, marshmallows and nuts."

"Excellent. The Valentine's and Easter products would be a piece of cake to come by."

"We could do an e-mail newsletter to keep people up-to-date on what holiday is coming up and some of the stuff we'll have in the store."

"I like it. A lot." He took a last bite of his roast beef sandwich, his expression thoughtful. "What if we sold some of the Estelle's House baked goods here?"

The students in Tony's independent living program ran a bakeshop in Apple Hill, creating all kinds of yummy treats under Rebecca's direction. "Simple stuff like coffee cake and turnovers."

"And I still want to get some of the kids over

here once the shop is open, expose them to another type of retail business."

They spent the rest of the lunch hour tossing ideas back and forth, feeding on each other's enthusiasm. Some of Jana's suggestions were goofy and outrageous, but Sam never made fun of them. He said they were brainstorming, just like he did with his books. He told her that anything goes when you're brainstorming, that there's no such thing as a stupid idea. That took some getting used to—that she could say anything she wanted and Sam wouldn't think she was a screwup.

After they'd cleaned up from lunch and Sam returned upstairs, Jana still felt that glow inside from his compliments. With paper towels and a bottle of spray cleaner, she tidied up the shop, bathroom and office as best she could, cutting through a few layers of dust. She knew she was overdoing it, working past her desperate need for an afternoon nap. But she wanted to please Sam, maybe get another one of those kudos from him.

When she finished around five, grubby and exhausted, she wanted nothing more than a shower and a good night's sleep. But when Sam showed up with yet another grin on his face and tugged at her arm to urge her upstairs, she did her best to put aside her cranky bad temper. As she climbed the stairs to the apartment, she saw that the contractors' truck was gone, leaving only the Villager behind the store.

When she first stepped inside the living room, she almost thought she was in the wrong place. The furniture had all been delivered. The living-room walls and kitchen cabinets all had a fresh coat of paint. The blinds were hung, with frilly little curtains across the top that were pulled back on either side.

"Come look in here," Sam said, the excitement clear in his voice.

He towed her along to the bathroom, showing her he'd hung the shower curtain they'd picked out, with its giant sunflowers on a sky-blue background. There was a brand-new toilet, and the spanking-new paint on the vanity matched the shower curtain's pale blue. Then in the bedroom, he'd made up the bed with the bedspread and comforter they'd bought the day before. The Eeyore lamp shone bravely on the night-stand beside the bed.

It was the silly lamp that did it for her. Eeyore, with his hangdog expression holding up the lightbulb, the lavender lampshade glowing with warmth.

"It's all so beautiful," she said. Then she col-lapsed on the foot of the bed and burst into tears.

She shouldn't have let him sit next to her. She should have jumped to her feet and run from the room instead of allowing him to put his arms around her. And she absolutely, positively never should have buried her face in his neck and bawled her eyes out.

He rubbed her back. "This whole crying thing is getting to be a real habit."

"When i-is it gonna s-stop?" she sobbed, embarrassed to the max and wanting to crawl under the bed.

"Maybe when your hormones settle down."

Except with his chin resting on top of her head, with his hands stroking her from shoulder to waist in slow arcs, she didn't think her hormones would ever mellow out. In fact, she thought maybe he was riling them up even worse.

He shifted—thank God he was pulling away—and she readied herself to stand up the moment he let go. But he didn't release her, just kept up that oh-so-pleasant pressure of his arms, his breathing long and deep against her ear.

Then he buried his mouth in her hair, the soft heat against her scalp sending her heart into a two-step. She couldn't see, could only feel— Good God, was he kissing her? His mouth moved along her hairline, down her brow, his lips settling at the sensitive place between her eyes. Her heart screamed in her chest, a hot, flaming phoenix.

Her hands clutched his sides so hard she was probably hurting him. She wanted his mouth on hers so badly she could hardly bear its absence.

Somehow, his T-shirt had scooted free of his jeans—had she done that?—and she could feel bare skin against her fingertips. She couldn't help herself—she stretched her fingers longer, drew them across that warm, taut smoothness.

He grew still, his mouth still on her, his breathing ragged. Then he just about pole-vaulted out of her arms. Stood over her, staring down, shock clearly on his face. She dropped her own gaze, mortified, again wishing she could creep under the bed out of sight. She thought of apologizing, then realized if she did, she'd have to admit she'd been groping him.

Before she could even draw a breath, he'd left the room. She heard him talking and realized he was on the phone ordering Chinese. Then she heard the front door open and close, and she figured he'd left.

But as she returned to the living room, he came back inside. Didn't quite look straight at her. "With the new stuff we brought over, you have a change of clothes for tomorrow, right?"

"Yeah." She'd seen it all hanging in her bedroom closet.

"Would you be okay sleeping here, then?"

"I'd like to sleep in my own place." She'd also like to do a total rewind on the past ten minutes.

"Good." He tucked his hands under his armpits, still not looking at her. "Dinner should be here in about thirty minutes. I gave the guy my credit card, so it's all paid for."

"Aren't you going to eat with me?"

"Not tonight. I have to…" He scanned the apartment, as if for an excuse. "Have to do stuff."

Then he grabbed up his sweater from the futon and walked to the door. For half a second, she thought he might give her a goodbye hug. But he must have been afraid she'd put the squeeze on him again if he did.

So he walked out, leaving her to mentally kick herself around the room like a soccer ball.

Chapter Seven

He'd been ready to kiss her, to touch her everywhere, to strip off her clothes and pull her down onto that bed. The sudden hurricane-force temptation had shocked him, the lightning-fast switch from comforting yet another Jana meltdown to raging lust. When he'd felt her inadvertent brush against his bare skin, it had both sent sensation jolting through him and knocked some sense into him. He'd skedaddled out of there as quickly as humanly possible.

And as luck would have it, the next morning fate stepped in to save him from himself. His agent's call woke him at 10:00 a.m.—long after he usually woke, but he'd been staring at the ceiling most of the night—and offered him a sanity-saving lifesaver. A writers' organization in Phoenix had lost its conference keynote speaker at the last minute to a nasty case of flu. Could he step in to give the opening speech tomorrow, Wednesday, and appear on a few discussion panels?

He gave a tentative yes, then called Tony and Rebecca to arrange for a few of the teens in their program to give Jana a hand in the shop while he was gone. Last thing he wanted was pregnant Jana schlepping around heavy boxes. Next, he called his accountant and insurance agent and set Jana up as an official employee with medical benefits. He arranged for the insurance agent to send the paperwork directly to Jana.

Reassured that Jana would have backup, he gave the conference organizers a thumbs-up and made his airline reservations. Then he dug the laptop computer and camera he'd promised Jana from his office closet. He'd wait until the afternoon to drop it off. By then Tony would have sent one of the boys over to help with the heavy lifting.

Sure enough, when Sam arrived at the shop at three-thirty, a familiar navy-blue sedan was parked out back. Tony had purchased the small, used four-door for the kids in the program to use. Two of them had turned up, a boy and a girl, and Jana had them opening boxes and itemizing the contents on a list.

When Jana first saw him, her expression was wary, but then she saw the laptop tucked under his arm. "Tell me that's for me. If I have to write one more thing by hand, my fingers will fall off."

"Set it up in the office or out here?" Sam asked.

"I think the Internet cable in the office is long enough to reach out here. Ray?" she called to the wiry, dark-haired boy digging through a cardboard box.

"I'm on it." He trotted off to the office, returning with a coil of blue cable.

Jana set up the computer beside the cash register on the front counter. Ray plugged in the cable. "I can get you set up," the boy told her.

"Thanks, Ray."

Stepping aside to let Ray work, she asked Sam, "Here to help?"

Guilt twinged inside him, but sexual attraction danced right next to guilt like a naughty younger brother. "Something came up." He told Jana about the writers' conference. "My agent piggybacked a Sunday-morning signing at a local bookstore, so I won't be back until that afternoon."

Was that relief he saw in her eyes? He felt even worse seeing it. That meant she'd figured out where his dirty little mind had been straying last night. Trying to be casual about it, he stepped back to give her some more breathing room.

"Can you check on the house while I'm gone?" He dug in his pocket for the extra set of keys he'd brought. "Bring in the mail, look through it. Open whatever you think needs attention."

"Sure." The keys might as well have been a snake, considering how gingerly she took them.

He gave her another foot of clearance. "I'd appreciate a call once a day. I can let you know what time works once I've seen the conference schedule."

"Call once a day. Check."

"And I set up medical insurance for you." He slipped a folded piece of printer paper from his back pocket. "This is a temporary card off their Web site."

"Thanks." She took the paper.

"Did you see an OB doctor in Portland?"

"At the free clinic." He saw a flicker of challenge in her eyes.

"Rebecca can probably recommend hers. I want you to make an appointment, ASAP."

She just nodded, not even arguing the point, which worried him even more. It was as if they were dancing around the room, keeping an invisible buffer between them. All because he'd stepped over the line last night and no doubt made her feel vulnerable.

He looked around him at the mismatched clutter arrayed across the shop floor. "You think you'll be able to sell some of this stuff on the Internet?"

She reached into the nearest box and pulled out a stuffed toy, a fluffy, big-eyed kitten. "Should be able to. Ian and I used to hit the garage sales on Saturdays. Then we'd sell the stuff online. My boss at the pub would let us use his computer to upload the pictures and set up the ads."

She clutched the kitten close, like a barrier. He wanted to tear his own head off as punishment for being responsible for that uneasiness in her. He glanced over at Ray, working at the computer, and the blond girl categorizing a box full of figurines. No way they could discuss this with the two teens there. It would just have to wait until he returned.

"When are you leaving?" she asked.

"Early tomorrow. I've got plenty to do to get ready, so I won't see you again until I get back."

He held his breath, trying to parse what he saw in her expressive face. Except she was holding her cards close to the vest now. If she was relieved or disappointed that he'd be away five days, he couldn't tell.

"The contractor should be done refinishing the floor in here by the time you get back." She stroked the silky fur of the stuffed kitten.

Damned if he didn't wish he was the one being stroked. "One small problem, though. My car is still at your place."

Sam didn't feel comfortable with leaving the kids here while Jana went with him to pick up her car. Not to mention the peril in being alone with her at his house, considering his current frame of mind.

"Ray, you have a license?"

The boy looked up from the computer. "Yeah."

"Ever ridden in a DeLorean?"

Now his eyes got as big as saucers. He just about fell over when Sam took him out back and he saw the stainless steel gull-wing. Ray lifted the door reverently and slid into the low-slung car, looking as if he'd died and gone to heaven.

A grin splitting his face, Ray sat in stunned silence as Sam took the curves back to his estate. When Sam was Ray's age, he would have given ten years of his life to ride in a car like the DeLorean. He felt a spark of joy giving a fellow foster kid that experience.

After Ray left in Jana's car, Sam packed, then checked his e-mail for updates from Melanie, the conference organizer. Based on Melanie's information, he wouldn't have to do much prep. He had a stock speech he gave at conferences, and he'd never given it in Phoenix. He'd print it out and give it a quick once-over on the plane. The panel discussions would require only a short bio. The rest of the five days he'd be schmoozing or maybe seeing a little of the Phoenix area.

Melanie had made it clear she'd be glad to show him around. Had made a point of mentioning she was single. Had even directed him to the photo on her Web site. The woman was a knockout, just his type.

But as he imagined shopping in Scottsdale or hiking Dreamy Draw, his mental movie starred Jana, not Melanie. It was he and Jana who would share the stark desert beauty. He'd show her the towering saguaro cactus, and she'd make jokes about their many-armed freakishness. It would be her hand he'd reach for to help her up the craggy boulders as they climbed to Piestewa Peak. Then once they'd reached the top, they'd stand together and admire the spill of scarlet in the sky as the sun set.

He had his hand on the phone, ready to call her, before he realized he couldn't invite Jana to Phoenix. Not until he got his head on straight with her. Bad enough he'd let his physical attraction to her get so out of control just because they'd spent a few days in close quarters. Who knew what would happen if he took her with him to a conference? Even if he booked her in her own room, she'd be only steps away.

He let go of the phone and slumped in his chair, then thought about how his libido was mucking up this great friendship with Jana.

He spent a few minutes feeling like a complete rat for even considering taking advantage of a mixed-up young woman who was pregnant and in need of his compassion, not a come-on.

He couldn't have Jana tonight, but he could have her alter ego. He opened up his notes document on his computer and spent the next couple of hours fleshing out his new character—he'd named her Lacey—and laying some meat on the bones of his new plot.

Lacey was still with him when he went to bed—early in deference to his 3:30 a.m. wake-up time—weaving herself into his dreams. In one fragment of sleeping fantasy, he made love to her, and in the midst of climax her face transformed from the one he'd imagined for his fictional character to Jana's.

The days Sam was gone moved so slowly for Jana that they just about went in reverse.

It was as if he fed her a continuous electrical charge when he was around, an energy main line she couldn't live without. His absence meant she fell back into herself, sinking into her self-doubt, reliving the mistakes and screwups that riddled her life. She pictured him surrounded by adoring fans, the beneficiaries of his charisma.

Despite her doldrums, she made great progress at the shop. She and Ray and Frances were able to group the stuff for sale so they could be sold in bunches rather than one item at a time, which would make the whole thing easier and quicker. The contractors worked on the floor Wednesday through Friday, sanding, staining and varnishing the beautiful old oak boards. She'd filled a legal pad with merchandise ideas for six months of holidays starting with their mid-April opening date. One full page listed name possibilities for the shop to replace the choice

Sam currently had registered with the court—The Christmas Store.

Like any of that would really distract her from her "Sam obsession." Here she was at Sam's house, Saturday afternoon, staring at the digital clock above his desk, watching it tick off the minutes until four o'clock—five o'clock Phoenix time. That was the slice of time between when his conference day ended and he was dragged out to dinner with those gaga fans he kept complaining about.

When the clock display read four, she forced herself to wait another few minutes before calling by playing another game of solitaire on Sam's computer, hand on the mouse instead of the phone. When it rang at five after four, she threw the mouse as she lunged to answer.

"Hey," she said, out of breath. "Thought I was doing the calling."

"I didn't want to take the chance I'd miss you.

They're transporting a bunch of us up to Sedona for dinner. The bus leaves in a couple minutes."

"I've always wanted to see Sedona." She said it lightly so he wouldn't think it meant a lot to her.

"I wish you were the one coming with me."

There was nothing light in the way he said it. The simple statement seemed heavy with meaning. *I miss you,* her mind cried out. There was a time she could have said that out loud— such as when she was twelve and he'd gone off to Utah for a summer—but now those words seemed to mean so much more.

So instead she talked about trivialities. "I bought the printer today. Put it on the Amex card." He'd given her the card during their shopping spree, having told her it was for business expenses.

"Anything interesting in the mail?"

She flipped through the stack, although she'd already looked it over. "A couple fan letters forwarded from your publisher. A royalty check from your agent. Did you check your voice mail? He called yesterday evening while I was here, and I heard part of the message."

"He had the details of that new movie option."

"Congratulations." As if she needed another reminder of how out of her league Sam was. Last week while they'd been so buddy-buddy, she'd forgotten the circles Sam usually traveled in. His latest film deal brought home the fact that, little sister or not, she was such a minor player in his life.

She heard a woman in the background call his name. "In a minute," he responded, his voice muffled.

Was that exasperation in his tone? Or just eagerness to be finished with Jana so he could join the woman and the others? Or maybe it would just be this woman and him in a private car while everyone else rode in the bus.

She would make herself crazy thinking that

way. "I'd better let you go." Her thumb hovered over the disconnect button.

"One more thing," he said, stopping her from hanging up. "I'd planned to land around three tomorrow afternoon. But Melanie's putting together a dinner for some of the local authors."

"Melanie?" Jealousy stabbed her, sharp as glass.

"The conference organizer. Should I stay another night? Or come home?"

Come home! Her heart all but yelled it. "Whatever you want."

"But do you—" He hesitated. "Is there anything I'm needed for at home?"

Was he asking if *she* needed him? She did, desperately. But she wasn't about to beg him. She had some pride. Plus she knew how important it was for him to keep promoting himself, even though he was Mr. Blockbuster Bestseller. Certainly more important than her wanting him home.

"Nothing going on I can't handle." The literal, if not emotional, truth.

She heard the woman again; then Sam made his apologies and signed off. As she stared at the phone, loneliness sat on her shoulder, crooning a sad little song in her ear.

Back at the apartment, she had little appetite for dinner, but she knew she had to eat. So she sautéed slices of chicken breast and tossed them with rigatoni, olive oil and Asiago cheese, then threw together a green salad to go with it. She ate as much as she could manage, remembering there were other needs besides hers at stake. Except that she didn't want to think about the baby and the inevitable loss she'd face when the adoption was final.

Sunday morning she woke to a brilliant blue sky and the glitter of frost kissing the pine trees outside. Bundling up in layers from the wardrobe Sam had bought her, she headed down the hill to Old Sacramento, a touristy section between the capitol and the Sacramento River.

She didn't like the sounds her engine was making as she drove down Highway 50 and considered turning back. But there were a half-dozen shops in Old Sac she wanted to check out. She'd arranged to speak with some of the owners about where they bought their merchandise, which companies were reliable sources and which weren't. In the back of her mind, she read Ian the riot act for talking her into selling her beautiful red Civic and buying this junker. He'd pocketed most of the profits in the transaction.

But the car got her safely to Old Sac, and she had a great time wandering around. Of course, it would have been way, way better exploring with Sam, asking his opinion about whether they should stock T-shirts and sweatshirts with seasonal slogans and sharing a chocolate-covered caramel apple from the candy place. But she took tons of notes and got plenty of good info. All the shopkeepers loved the idea of a holiday shop and thought the location up in El Dorado County's Apple Hill was a great one. She had such a good time that she didn't get back to the car until nearly three.

The noise started up again just as she hit the interchange between Interstate 5 and Highway 50. She did okay for another ten miles or so; then the engine started bucking and surging. With a death grip on the wheel, she pressed on, hoping and praying that the evil spell her life seemed to be under might not hold for just this once.

Sam was jammed in the jet aisleway between a stout woman and a couple of squirmy kids when his phone rang. He had to wriggle past his carry-on to free the cell from his back pocket, where he'd shoved it after turning it back on. When he saw the caller ID, his heart shifted into overdrive.

"Jana? Are you okay?"

"No." Her voice shook and terror ratcheted up another notch. "I'm stuck." He heard the roar of what sounded like a semi. "On the freeway."

"How— Never mind. Where are you?" As she described which exits on the freeway she was stuck between, dread oozed up inside him. The flight attendants still hadn't opened the damn door.

"Stay in the car, Jana. Call 911. I'll get a tow truck." The door finally open, Sam inched forward along the aisle. "I should be there in thirty minutes. Don't you move from that car." He refused to let himself imagine Jana walking along the freeway, exposed to the fast-moving traffic.

Once he was in the Jetway, he punched a preset on his phone for his auto club. More juggling of his carry-on to retrieve his wallet, but he got a tow truck ordered. He grabbed his checked bag the moment it popped out onto the conveyer belt, then took off like a tight end through the crowd.

He topped the speed limit by only ten miles per hour, whipping in and out of the light Sunday-afternoon traffic. By the time he pulled his Prius onto the shoulder behind Jana's junker, the tow driver was there and she was standing safely beside the freeway embankment.

He threw his arms around her, holding her close, feeling her heart thunder against his. "You're not driving that car anymore."

She tipped her head back, a faint wash of color flagging her pale cheeks. "I suppose you're going to let me use the DeLorean."

He couldn't help his grin. "In your dreams. You can borrow the Prius."

She buried her face in his chest. "Thank you for being here when I needed you."

He thought his heart would leap from his chest. "I'm just so glad you're safe. That the baby's safe."

Seeing the tow driver getting ready to roll the old junker up onto the bed of his wrecker, Sam let go of Jana. They got the rest of her belongings transferred to his Prius.

As they merged back onto Highway 50, Sam could see she was still shaken by the breakdown. Her throat worked as she seemed to struggle against tears. "I thought you weren't coming home until tomorrow."

So did he, until he found himself packing like an automaton this morning, loading up the rental car so he could head for Sky Harbor Airport the moment his bookstore appearance ended. All the while he spoke to the crowd of readers, he could think of nothing but seeing Jana again. Thank God he'd listened to his instincts.

His gaze linked with hers, just for an instant

before he returned his attention to the road. But with just that brief visual contact, realization hit him with the force of a skipload of bricks.

What he was feeling for Jana—it was the same single-minded obsession he'd felt for Faith when he'd first met her. And for Shawna before Faith and Cyndy before Shawna. He was laying his usual modus operandi on Jana, as if she was just one in a long line of women he professed to love and then later left.

Panic filled him. Was that what all this sexual attraction was about? Him taking himself down that same ambush-riddled path to disaster? Was there some twisted part of himself that wanted to turn his relationship with Jana into something physical so he could travel that same rutted road before discarding her?

No way. He wasn't going there. Because Jana was better than that. She was his friend, his sister. If he let himself follow his usual habitual pattern with Jana, she could be lost to him forever. His gut burned at the thought.

Jana pulled him from his dark musing. "You want to stop in at the shop? See what we got done while you were gone?"

Of course he did. Because now that he was back home, with Jana again, he wanted nothing more than to be with her.

He had to take a step back. Get some space, clear his head.

He leapt to the first excuse that popped into his mind. "Actually, during the flight I got some ideas on the new book. I want to get them down before I lose them."

"How about dinner, then?"

A fist of longing settled in his chest. Spending an hour sharing a meal with Jana would be a little piece of paradise. "Too much to do. Unpacking and laundry and…stuff. In fact, I've been thinking…if the kids have been working out at the shop—"

"They've been great. They hardly let me lift a finger."

"I want to get started on this book early. While everything's fresh in my mind. Which means you might not be seeing much of me for a while."

A few beats of silence settled in the car before she spoke again. "Okay. No problem."

She said the words so casually, as if it didn't matter to her at all that he was retreating back into his shell. As if she could take or leave his company.

He pressed on past the ache inside him. "You can access my e-mail from the shop. Follow up on fan mail, let my agent know about any speaking requests."

"Sure."

"And, you know, I'll pop in sometimes. It's not like you won't see me at all."

"Whatever, Sam. We'll be fine." She sounded as if she meant it.

He drove straight to his place, then after he'd retrieved his luggage from the trunk, watched her drive away. He stood on his front porch a long time, imagining her wending her way back to the security gate, then passing through. Wishing he could call her back.

Then he walked inside his lonely house and faced an endless time without Jana.

Chapter Eight

If Jana thought those five days Sam was in Phoenix had slogged by, that was nothing compared to the rest of January and all of February. It didn't help that it poured like Noah's flood twenty-six out of the forty-odd days during his absence. At the tail end of February, a cold front from Canada dropped in on Apple Hill with subfreezing temperatures and six inches of snow.

She kept herself busy with the shop, handling Sam's snail- and e-mail, forwarding on whatever she thought needed his attention. By previous agreement, she'd pick up the mail that arrived at the post-office box he kept for fans, leaving the correspondence that arrived at the house for him to deal with. He'd also provided her with a stack of autographed books, author copies for donating to worthy fund-raising causes.

So, while they talked during those long weeks, by phone and e-mail, occasionally face-to-face at the shop, the conversations were short and sweet, leaving her aching for more. It was like when she was a kid and Sam's visits to Estelle's were few and far between. Sam was the only bright spot in her life.

She distracted herself with Frances's and Ray's antics, with visits to the Estelle's House ranch. At first she thought Tony would never forgive her for deserting him to take off with Ian. But after a couple of deluge-soaked weekends helping Rebecca and her students clean the bakeshop kitchen and dining room, he started to come around.

The last Sunday in February, while Ray, Frances and the other teens whiled away the rainy afternoon working on pie dough in the bakeshop's big commercial kitchen, Rebecca and Jana put their feet up in the dining room. With the bakeshop on hiatus until April, only a couple of the eight-foot folding tables were set up in the dining room, each one ringed with chairs. The rest of the tables and chairs were neatly stacked to one side.

"I like the pictures," Jana said, admiring the photos that filled one wall. The portraits featured the ten participants in the Estelle's House program's first session.

"Tony thought it would be a nice tradition to put the students' pictures up once they graduate." Rebecca turned from the photo gallery to eye Jana's still mostly flat belly. "I'm only a month further along than you.

How come I already look like I'm carrying a watermelon and you're still svelte as ever?"

"How come you have actual boobs and mine look more like apricots?" Jana stared down at her chest. "If I can't get a good bust out of this, what good is pregnancy anyway?"

Rebecca smiled, but Jana saw a tinge of something sadder in her friend's eyes. "How are you and Sam getting along?" she asked.

"Great. I never see him." She'd meant to say it as a joke, as if she preferred their separation. But her throat tightened up at the end.

Of course, Rebecca heard that little catch. "What's going on with you two?"

"Nothing. He's busy with his book. I'm busy with the shop. I work for him, Rebecca. There's nothing else between us than that." She did better that time, keeping the words matter-of-fact. "I mean, yeah, we're friends, but that's all."

"He seemed thrilled that you'd come back."

Jana laughed. "You don't have to exagger-
ate to make me feel better."

Rebecca fixed her steady gaze on Jana.
"He's coming this evening. That's why the
kids are working so hard on making the
perfect apple pie."

"He never mentioned it."

Jana could see the uneasiness in Rebecca's
face. "He's been having dinner over here
most Sundays."

That knocked the air clean out of Jana's
lungs. Because she was here so late some
weekends, she'd shared Saturday-night dinner
with the Estelle's House crowd and the occasional Friday night as well. But she'd always
headed home by four or so on Sunday.

A sharp pain curled up in her stomach.
"He's been waiting for me to leave?"

"No," Rebecca said. "At least not the way
you think."

"What other way is there to think about it? He

stays away when he knows I'm here, then shows up when I'm gone."

"Jana." Rebecca took Jana's hand, held it against her round belly. "I think Sam's pretty confused."

"And I'm not?" She patted her stomach. "Kinda got a few things on my mind myself."

"He's just always found it easier to keep people at arm's length."

"Tell me something I don't know." She flung her hands out in frustration. "I wish I'd never asked him for help. I wish I'd just gone some place in Portland, found a doctor who would—"

A hand might as well have closed around her throat. She couldn't say the words, couldn't even allow herself to think them. She stroked her belly in apology.

"Maybe I should have tried harder with Ian to get him to step up to the plate. Then I never would have had to dump my problems in Sam's lap."

Rebecca put an arm around her shoulders. "Sam's glad you came to him. Glad you're nearby. He might not want to let people get too close, but he likes to know that those he cares about are okay."

Jana knew Rebecca was right, but the fact that Sam seemed to be actively avoiding her still stung. She started to get up. "I guess I should get going. Before he gets here."

Rebecca's hand on her shoulder kept Jana in her chair. "Stay for dinner." When Jana tried again to rise, Rebecca didn't let up the pressure of her hand. "You might have Tony convinced to let bygones be bygones, but I think I still have some payback coming from you for deserting me last September. This is the first meal the kids are preparing for Sam entirely on their own. I need you here to soothe nerves."

Almost as if Rebecca had planned it that

way, one of the girls—Frances maybe—
shrieked in dismay from the kitchen. With a
grin, Rebecca pushed to her feet and gave
Jana a hand up. Arms linked, they walked into
the kitchen to see what culinary creation
needed saving from the jaws of catastrophe.

Sam's first heads-up that Jana might still be
at the ranch came when he detoured into town
to see if the Prius was parked behind the shop.
She could have been out running errands
somewhere—wondering about where she
might be and who she might be with gave him
heartburn—but he figured it was most likely
she was still hanging out with Rebecca. So
when his candy apple–red 1968 Mustang
slogged through the puddles in the ranch's
gravel parking lot and his headlights picked
out the Prius alongside Tony's pickup, he
knew there'd be a moment of reckoning
served up with his dinner tonight.

Parking his car with plenty of clearance on either side, he trotted across the wet, muddy gravel toward the warm glow of the bakeshop. The kitchen door was closest, so he entered that way, then wished he hadn't when he saw the mass hysteria playing out. Two of the teens were screaming at each other at the stove, two others with a glaze of panic in their eyes were garnishing plates on the center island and Ray was up to his elbows in dirty pots.

Rebecca spared Sam one quick glance, then called to Jana, "Get him out of here."

Jana grabbed his arm and towed him away, slipping through the madly moving bodies. After so many weeks of self-imposed exile from her, having Jana's hands on him was just about sending his circuits into overload.

"Sorry. Freak-out time. It was all going well until Liz put orange juice instead of lemon in the chicken piccata."

He unzipped his rain jacket. Before he could

stop her, Jana was behind him, helping him off with it, her fingers brushing the nape of his neck, then the length of his arms. He shuddered, hoping she'd assume it was a chill from the icy deluge outside.

She nabbed his hat, as well, then pushed a lock of hair back from his eyes. Still recovering from the contact on the back of his neck, the near-instantaneous graze across his forehead poleaxed him. He stood frozen as she crossed the room, hooking his hat and jacket on a coatrack with several others.

Even the warning that she was here hadn't been enough to build any defense against her. Not when he'd spent the past six weeks alternating thoughts of his new book with fantasies of her. Write a paragraph, think of Jana, write a sentence, imagine Jana, type a word…

It was a testament to his professionalism that he'd gotten as many pages written as he had. But that was likely because his fictional journalist, Lacey Willits, might as well have been Jana. Every moment he wrote about Lacey, he felt as if he were spending time with Jana.

"Anything I can do?" he asked.

Busywork might keep his mind off how incredible Jana looked in jeans and that thick wool sweater, as vivid red as the Mustang outside. She'd never been much for makeup, but she and Rebecca must have spent some girlie-girl time together, because she wore lip gloss just a shade lighter than the sweater.

And damn his overactive imagination, he wanted to kiss the lipstick off. See what it tasted like, how her mouth tasted. Feel the changing curves of her body under that sweater.

"Just sit," she said, pointing to the head of the tables set end-to-end. "Tonight you're not a helper bee—you're a customer. It's our job to please you."

Then she returned to the kitchen, leaving him gasping for air. He sat himself down, taking a slice of French bread from the basket in front of him and slathering it with butter just to give his hands something to do.

Within a few minutes, the teens started ferrying out the main dish—chicken à l'orange instead of chicken piccata. They served him first, then quickly set plates around the table. In far less time than he thought possible, considering the insanity of a few minutes ago, everyone was seated— eight teens, Rebecca, Tony, Estelle and Jana.

Jana sat to his right, her knees bumping against his. She wasn't nudging him on purpose, nor was she trying to avoid touching him. She kept smiling, laughing, joking with him and with the others around the table, her expression never changing whether her knees were in contact with his or not. He, on the other hand, could barely focus on his meal, waiting for her to touch him again, holding his breath until she moved away.

He praised the meal and ate every bite, although considering his distraction, he could have been eating pabulum. He didn't want the kids thinking he didn't appreciate their efforts. It was not their fault that Jana had stayed for dinner and he just couldn't handle being near her.

At seven-thirty, after they'd all finished their apple pie à la mode and the kids had started the cleanup, Sam pushed back from the table, ready to make his escape. Jana was in the kitchen with Rebecca and the others. He could give them a quick wave through the pass-through and leave by way of the dining-room door.

But he'd barely raised his hand to give his goodbyes when Jana called out, "Sam, I need to talk to you."

She wove through the busy students toward him, snagging his arm and all but perp-walking him outside to the front of the bakeshop. The rain had let up, the clouds gusting away to reveal a sliver of moon overhead. Neither the moon nor the lights inside provided much illumination, leaving him and Jana in the mysterious dark.

Whatever imperative had driven her to bring him out here seemed to have stalled. She kept glancing over at him, whether to gather courage or to abort her mission, he wasn't sure. He didn't exactly want to give her encouragement, but if she had something to say, he felt he owed it to her to give her the time to speak her piece.

There was a wood and wrought-iron park bench set outside, tucked under the overhanging eave. Sam tested the seat with his palm and found it was dry to the touch. "Sit?"

She settled on one end, hands tucked between her thighs, no doubt for warmth. He was sure he could do a better job of warming her hands; in fact, he could slip his hands around hers between her legs and—

He sliced off that notion with a mental machete. Sitting beside Jana, he shoved his own hands under his armpits to keep them out of mischief. "Well?"

She took a good, long breath. "Here's the thing. I am grateful to the max for everything you've done for me. The way you've taken me in, given me a job and place to stay."

Something about the tone of her voice thrust a sudden crazy idea into his mind. This was the big farewell. With all the work Jana had been doing here at the ranch, Tony had realized what a find she was and had eked out a job and living quarters for her. Or even worse—Sam's heart just about stopped beating in his chest—Ian had been in touch with her again. He'd had an epiphany about what an ass he'd been and now was ready to be a father.

His panic went up another notch as she continued. "That gratitude is what kept me from saying anything before now. But it just isn't right to keep going the way we have been."

He would start hyperventilating any minute now. He could cope with her returning here to the ranch—he'd still see her often enough. But if she went back to Ian, moved off to the Midwest or God knew where…

He wanted to grab her, to keep her here, but he just kept his hands where they were. Still, the frantic energy inside had him bouncing his legs, shaking the bench and Jana as well, no doubt. But he couldn't sit still.

"You have to do what you think is right," he told her, his voice sounding rough to his ears.

"Exactly." She turned toward him. Her face was more shadow than light, her expression impossible to decipher. "So here's the deal."

He gulped in a breath. Dug his fingernails into his sides.

Then she turned him upside down again. "It's time to cut the crap."

"What crap?"

She waved a finger at him. "Stop hiding from me, avoiding me, turning yourself into a hermit because you've got some brainless idea it's best for me. We are friends." She poked him in the arm with each word. "We do best when we spend at least a little time together, talking, arguing, sharing good Mexican and bad Chinese. If you've gotta work, you know I understand. Because I've got plenty of my own work to do. But during the in-between times, we can both squeeze in a little time for each other."

His legs stopped bouncing as he struggled to take in what she'd just said. "You want to spend more time with me."

She gave him a sharp nod. "Because I need your input on the shop. Because I'm not sure I know how to answer every fan letter you get. Because I just plain enjoy your company. And I'm tired of sitting around at home alone because you have some goofy idea you need to set me free to spread my wings on my own." She flapped her hands in parody.

That she wasn't leaving was good. That she hadn't figured out why he'd been staying away—that his physical attraction for her threatened to mess up everything good about their relationship—was stellar. He'd missed her so desperately these past several weeks. He was such a self-centered SOB that it hadn't even crossed his mind that she might miss him, too.

"Come here," he said, reaching across the bench for her. He wrapped her in his arms, tucking her head under his chin. He felt the flare of attraction, but he blanked it as best he could and just let himself enjoy her nearness.

God, he cared so much for her. She was his best pal, the one he could tell anything to. Someone he could trust with his secrets, if he ever felt ready to share them. The whole sexual thing was an aberration, the side effect of a couple of months without a significant other. It was probably time to start scouting for a new girlfriend so he could stop those inappropriate thoughts.

Her breath on his throat grew warmer, her mouth moist against his skin. He wove his fingers into her hair, enjoying the length of the silky strands, the way they tickled his palms. He brought his other hand up to cradle her jaw, tipped her head back so he could see her face and trailed his thumb along her lips to see if he could make her smile.

Her dark eyes seemed enormous, rich with enigma and riddle. He brought his mouth gently down on the lids of her eyes as they fluttered closed, wishing he could solve the puzzle of Jana with that slight touch. She sighed and he spread his hands wider, feeling her heat soak into him. Then his lips drifted lower, along her high cheekbone, across her cheek, zigzagging back toward her mouth.

He only wanted to know her better. To understand what lay in his friend's heart. Tease out what she kept hidden inside. It wasn't a kiss. It was an exploration, a discovery.

He heard, he felt her sigh the moment his mouth covered hers. Felt her lips soften, felt them part. Tasted the first damp moisture within with the tip of his tongue. Dipped inside ever so slightly with a quick sweep.

He thought he'd come apart right there, just from a kiss. But, no, it wasn't a kiss. Just a touch, just an exploration.

A blast of wind spattered them both with the runoff dripping from the roof. He let Jana go and rose clumsily, tangling his feet on the leg of the bench. Groping for balance, he slapped his hand on one of the broad windows that fronted the bakeshop. Inside, Rebecca was just turning off the dining-room light switch, plunging him and Jana into a deeper darkness.

He could see the faintest glint in Jana's eyes. "I didn't mean to... I wasn't trying to..." He tried to order his thoughts. "Hell, I don't know what I was doing."

Silence swirled around them with the breeze. "What I said about more time together—"

"I know. That wasn't what you meant." He put his hand out for her. "Ready to go?"

"Let me grab my purse. I'll get your jacket and hat."

When she came back, she kept a buffer zone between them. She kept her goodbye hug brief, tentative, and he could feel her holding her breath. He wanted to try again to explain what he'd done on that bench, but he wasn't exactly clear on the concept himself. Yeah, his libido had been wagging its naughty little tail, whispering suggestions. But there had been something more, something deeper in those charged moments.

It wasn't as if she was a lover. But it was a

hell of a lot more than friendship. And how that interlude would fit into the world he and Jana shared he had no damn idea.

Chapter Nine

The first few weeks of March, Jana saw so much of Sam that she would have thought they'd get tired of each other or start to bicker about stupid things. But those twenty-something days were like some kind of magical interlude. The last of her morning sickness had vanished. She'd never smiled so often, never laughed as much, never told so many really awful jokes in her life. All that time, she kept looking over her shoulder for her old companion, disaster, but so far he was a no-show.

Sam would work on his book for several hours starting early in the morning, while Jana and one or two of the teens would set up the display shelves or unpack merchandise that was arriving daily. Then he'd join her, helping the teens with the heavy work that he absolutely refused to let her do.

They'd all have lunch; then she and Sam would often spend the afternoon brainstorming ideas for the shop or plot complications for his book. Or they'd head down the hill to run errands, sometimes stopping for dinner and a movie before returning home. If she made him dinner at the apartment, they'd play cards afterward or watch some television.

With all the conversation that flew fast and furious between them, there was one topic of discussion they wouldn't touch with a fifty-foot pole. That night at the ranch. Her in his arms. His kiss.

A part of her wondered if she'd imagined the

whole thing. Another part, that wishful-thinking part, wondered what it had meant. Because although she'd burned from head to toe with the feel of his mouth on hers, there was something about his touch that had seemed…well, not chaste exactly. But not really sexual. There had been something more to it. Something deeper, more complex. Something she most definitely didn't understand.

But he hadn't shown even a smidgen of interest in a repeat performance. She told herself that was good, that the last thing she wanted was to follow in her mother's foot-steps. But some nights, as she lay in bed alone, the longing for Sam just about killed her.

Now, sitting at the apartment's kitchen table, her feet up on the second vinyl dinette chair, Jana stared into her peppermint tea, replaying for the millionth time every moment of Sam's kiss. She was alone this morning, the teens all too busy preparing for the big Easter carnival and egg hunt at the ranch. The fund-raiser was scheduled for Saturday, the 27th of March, and only two days away. The kids had been going crazy baking, building game booths and decorating. Jana and Sam had been able to get them a good deal on the decorations and game prizes, but Rebecca was insisting the teens do everything else themselves. Which left Jana out of the loop.

There were a few things she could have done downstairs this morning, but it just wasn't the same without Sam. He usually showed up by noon; it was a quarter after.

She moved to the living-room window to watch for him to pull up out back. Holding the mug of tea, her gaze out at the pine trees shielding Highway 50 from her sight, she almost missed it. She wouldn't have even known what she was feeling, if Rebecca, a month ahead of her, hadn't described it a few weeks ago.

"Oh," she whispered, setting the mug of tea

down on the windowsill. She stared down at her belly, at five months now pooching out far enough that no one could miss the fact that she was pregnant. She held her breath, afraid breathing would keep her from feeling it again.

Then she felt it, clear as day. Like a bubble inside her, kind of a swish. Too subtle to feel or see from the outside yet. Not like it would be later, according to what Rebecca had told her.

She plastered herself against the window, willing Sam to come. When he finally arrived five minutes later, she flung open the door and hurried out to the landing.

"Sam!" she all but screamed down at him as he climbed from the Mustang.

He slammed the car door and raced up the steps. "What's the matter? Are you okay?"

She smiled so he wouldn't worry, so full of joy she could have floated off the landing. "I felt the baby move."

A mix of expressions danced across his face,

so quickly she couldn't figure them all out. But happiness settled last, and he threw his arms around her. "That's great, fantastic."

As they walked inside, a dose of reality slapped Jana upside the head. Her joy faded even as the little minibun tumbled again inside her.

She sat on the sofa as Sam shut the door. "It's probably not such a great idea getting so excited about the baby moving."

He settled on the armchair beneath the window. "Maybe not."

She curved her fingers around her belly. "It's just hard sometimes to think about it. Watching the baby grow all these months. Then saying goodbye."

He leaned forward, elbows on his knees. "You don't have to, Jana."

"Nothing's changed. I still don't have a dime to my name except what you give me."

"You work for that money."

"I do." As hard as she could. And she'd saved every penny she could, a part of her still wishing she could build enough of a nest egg to keep her baby.

But not even those tight-fisted savings would last beyond a few months. She'd still be scraping by for food and diapers for the baby. She couldn't begin to afford day care, which would allow her to work. Wouldn't it be selfish to raise her child in poverty just because she wasn't strong enough to give it up?

The baby moved yet again, as if to express an opinion. But darned if Jana could figure out what that was. She only knew she didn't want to think about it right now.

"Did you want to go through the Christmas catalog again, finalize our order?"

The holiday season might be more than eight months away, but it would be a big one for the store. She wanted all the details nailed down way in advance. Especially since she probably wouldn't be here past September.

It was as if the last of the air seeped out of her little balloon of happiness. September was a mere five months away. By then the baby would be born. And gone, living with another family. The balloon went flat.

Sam had been looking off into the middle distance, his thoughts impenetrable. When he zeroed in on her again and said, "Why not?" it took her a few seconds to remember the question he was answering.

They went downstairs, the brisk early spring breeze stealing under Jana's roomy long-sleeved T-shirt. She wrapped her arms around her middle, wanting to keep her belly warm.

Melancholy descended again as she waited for Sam to unlock the back door. Would she have a chance to hold her baby? Should she? Maybe it would be best if she never saw it.

"I like the sign," Sam said as they walked inside.

The lighted window sign, spelling out Celebration Station in colorful neon, had been delivered and installed yesterday. A couple weeks ago, when Sam was still digging in his heels about changing the shop's name, she wasn't sure if they'd get the sign finished before their April 10 opening. But then one night, he'd abruptly changed his mind, and Jana was able to get the wheels turning with the neon artist.

They sat together in the office, flipping through the catalog. Sam nodded in all the right places, even threw in a comment or two, but Jana could see his mind was somewhere else. The feel of the baby's movements still so fresh, her heart still tender and grieving, she wanted all of Sam here with her. She thought of grabbing him and shaking him, demanding he pay attention to her, now. Then she gave herself a mental kick in the butt and told herself to buck up.

They were almost finished anyway; then they could go get some lunch. She reached into the filing cabinet and pulled out a file folder. She'd been clipping photos of decorated rooms from old magazines for the past several weeks.

She spread the pictures across the desk. "I was thinking we'd set the store up kind of like a living room. One big Christmas tree in the corner with presents piled underneath. Garland and ribbons everywhere, small tables set up with seasonal tablecloths, Christmassy shades on the lamps, standup Santas and snowmen. Of course, everything on display would be available for sale."

It was as if she'd lassoed him and brought him back from outer space. He riveted his gaze on those happy, gorgeous photos, the rooms perfectly decorated for Christmas.

She'd clipped each page for only one or two ideas. They were mostly way too busy for her taste. But she might as well have waved a magic wand over Sam's head. She could see that from his soft smile, the light in his eyes, he loved every overdone bit of glitter in the pictures.

He picked them up, one by one, taking his time, his gaze moving from one feature on the page to the next. Once he'd examined them all way more closely than Jana had ever expected, he went back to the second one in the array.

"This is what I want," he said, setting the magazine page in Jana's hands.

It was the most garish of the bunch, a riot of vivid color. Most of the others were themed— all silver, all gold, variations on bells, Santas, snowmen. But that particular room had been decorated with just about every Christmas symbol on the planet, many of them animated. Reds and greens and blues and purples screamed from the page. It was like a child's fantasy of Christmas.

"A little over the top, don't you think?" Not to mention a headache to set up in the shop the size of Celebration Station. She got vertigo just thinking about all those animated pieces moving at once.

"It's perfect," Sam said, a familiar stubborn set to his jaw. "This is how I want to decorate the store."

"Okay," Jana agreed, drawing out the syllables. What did it matter, anyway? She wouldn't be here for the final setup. "Ready for lunch?"

Now guilt flickered across his face. "I have plans."

A boulder of disappointment dropped in her stomach. "An appointment with your accountant?" With the April 15 tax deadline approaching, maybe there were some details they had to iron out.

"Not my accountant. Someone else." He wouldn't look at her. That set off alarm bells she tried to ignore.

She ordered herself to breathe. "No biggie. I can throw together something here. Or maybe go up to Mae's Diner."

He checked his watch, pushed to his feet. "How about dinner instead?"

How about you tell me who you're seeing? "I've been craving spaghetti and meatballs."

"Great." He gave her a kiss on the forehead absentmindedly, like he used to when she'd been a twerp and he a grown man. Then he was out the door without so much as a look back.

She stacked up the magazine pages and stuffed them back into the folder, with Sam's choice on top. Without him for company, she didn't have much of an appetite. But she heated a can of tomato soup and made a peanut butter and jelly sandwich and finished both as if they were medicine she had to take.

A quick survey of her fridge told her she'd need to go to the market for some ground beef for the meatballs. If she went down to Placerville, she could spend a little time browsing the shops. It'd be kind of lonely without Sam, but she ought to get used to doing stuff without him. Friend or not, they weren't exactly attached at the hip.

Deciding to save her marketing for later so the meat wouldn't spoil, she drove into Placerville, parked the Prius and headed up the north side of Main Street. The late-March sunshine spilled down yellow as butter, warming the breeze, cheering Jana despite her longing for Sam. Maybe she'd get herself some gelato from the little place she and Sam often stopped in for lunch.

She'd just reached the café, had been about to turn for the entrance when a familiar silhouette caught her eye. Sitting by the window, his back to her, was Sam. She recognized the forest-green T-shirt he'd been wearing, of course, but even if he'd changed clothes, she had those broad shoulders memorized.

And opposite him, her pretty face animated as she spoke, was a woman.

It was as if someone had poured hot oil over her, inside and out. Sam had made plans for lunch with someone else, hadn't wanted to tell her with whom. He had every right to date someone new, but why wouldn't he just tell her? She might not have wanted to know, but better fair warning than this surprise.

Calm down, idiot. This could be anyone— a fellow author, a friend, his accountant's married daughter. There didn't have to be anything special between them.

But then Sam reached across the table and took the woman's hand. Held it in both of his. Cradled it as if it was precious, the most wonderful gift. Jana could imagine the way Sam was looking at the woman. It was the way she wanted Sam to look at her.

Jana tried to drag her gaze away, but it was as if her eyes were stuck on the image, like a movie on pause. She studied the woman's face, her dark wavy hair, the blue eyes. The black Irish look of her, the familiarity of her smile.

It hit her with the force of a wrecking ball. This wasn't Sam's new love. And no distant cousin either. She looked so much like Sam that Jana would bet a million dollars this was his sister.

His real sister. Not a fake, you're-just-like-a-sister figure like Jana. The woman in the restaurant was Sam's blood relation, a real link to his past. Someone that would mean about a hundred times more to Sam than Jana did.

Jana racked her brains—what had Sam said her name was? Maddie? He'd only mentioned her the one time, when he'd come over to Estelle's after yet another breakup. Jana was seventeen at the time, during her madly-in-love-with-Sam phase. Sam had been a little drunk, and he'd let slip that he had a sister named Maddie whom he hadn't seen in years.

And here he was meeting her again in the flesh, but he didn't say one word about it to Jana. Why was that? Why not share that good news? Maybe because now that he had the real McCoy, he didn't need a pale imitation. Probably this afternoon, when he'd been so distracted, was just a taste of how he would start withdrawing from Jana's life.

No wonder Sam was in another world. He was planning to meet his sister. That had to be big for him, huge. Way more significant than spending yet another lunch with Jana Not-Really-His-Sister McPartland.

Jana ordered her feet to move, backing away from the café. She'd lost her taste for gelato. Had no heart for window-shopping. She'd just go to the market, then head home again.

Pulling into the supermarket parking lot, she

tried to push down the pain inside her. But it stayed lodged in her chest all the time she shopped, all during the drive home, the entire afternoon while she made dinner for Sam. A dinner he would probably wish he was sharing with Maddie instead of Jana.

Sam stared across the table at his sister, no doubt a goofy grin on his face, and wished to hell he'd brought Jana along. But he hadn't known how it would go today, if it would work out or be awkward and uncomfortable, so he'd thought it would be better to fly this one solo.

Still he'd hated to leave her behind. The past few weeks had been great, better than great. His book was just about writing itself, the time he spent with Jana energizing his creativity. And although that zing that shimmered between him and her never went away, he'd managed to box away that night at the ranch, the kiss outside the dining room, and not obsess about it. Not too much anyway.

"God, I'm glad I e-mailed you," Sam said to his sister for about the hundredth time.

And for about the hundredth time, she smiled at him across the table. "Me, too."

Other than when they were eating lunch, they'd barely let go of each other's hands. He hung on, a little afraid she'd disappear, that the past hour and a half had been a dream.

"I wish things had been different, Sam. That Aunt Barbara hadn't kept us apart the way she did."

"I wish I hadn't been such a jerk when you contacted me five years ago." He was still kicking himself over that, regretting the time lost in getting to know his sister.

He couldn't wait to introduce Maddie to Jana. He was sure Maddie would love Jana. That they'd instantly click the way he and Jana had all those years ago.

That pleasant prospect was sidetracked by the question that had been lurking in the back of Sam's mind. The one he didn't know if he'd ever get a chance to ask. The one he wasn't even sure he wanted answered.

He took a breath. "When Mom left, those days we were alone…"

He saw the sympathy in Maddie's eyes. "That was a long time ago, Sam."

"I just need to know," he went on before he could chicken out. "How much do you remember?"

"I was two years old," she reminded him.

"So you don't remember anything?"

"No, except…" Her brow furrowed. "The bathwater running."

Sam's stomach clenched as the memories flooded him. Maddie's fever spiking, the cool bath the only thing he could think of to bring it down. He'd left her for only a minute, less than a minute.

Maddie must have seen something of his inner torment, because she gave his hand a squeeze. "We both came out okay, Sam. What does it matter what happened twenty-five years ago?"

The server returning with his credit card saved him from having to answer. As he signed the slip, Maddie asked a question of her own. "Have you ever looked for her?"

He didn't have to ask who she meant. "No."

"But haven't you ever wondered—"

"No, I haven't." A big fat lie. Few days went by that his mother didn't at least drift into the periphery of his mind.

"It would be nice to know," Maddie said quietly.

Darius could find her, probably in a heartbeat. But that was yet another question he'd just as soon leave unanswered.

They walked along Main Street. "That woman you're helping. Jana."

"What about her?"

"To take her in like that, to help her get through her pregnancy… I kind of wondered if there was more between you."

"More?" They stopped at the crosswalk, waiting for traffic to clear. "More like what?"

"The way your face lights up when you talk about her, it reminds me of Matthew. He looks at me that way sometimes."

"Matthew, your fiancé?" He put a hand on her arm as they stepped into the street. "As in, the guy who's madly in love with you?"

When they reached the other side where their cars were parked, she stopped him, looked up at him. "Are you in love with her?"

He went hot, then cold, then hot again. "No! Yes, I think the world of her. Like I do Estelle, and my friend Tony. But, no, I'm not in love with her."

Of course he wasn't. Because if he fell in love with Jana, it wouldn't be long before he fell out again. Then he wouldn't want her in his life anymore and would send her away. He couldn't bear the thought of seeing Jana leave.

The contradicting thoughts collided with each other, leaving him even more confused. He tried to figure out how to explain things to Maddie as they stopped beside his Mustang. "When I first met Jana fourteen years ago, my life was pretty upside down. I'd been on my own for three years, was still scared to death I'd end up on the street. School was way harder than I thought it would be."

Maddie leaned against the car beside him. "I wish I could've been there for you."

"Aunt Barbara never would have let you."

"Still…" Her arms wrapped around her, Maddie stared down at the sidewalk. "I don't remember much about when Aunt Barbara sent you away. I wondered what happened to my brother. But I was so young, I kind of forgot you for a while."

"She didn't talk about me at all?" It shouldn't matter after all this time. But it cut so deep that he'd been discarded that way, even though he'd been such a juvenile delinquent.

"Just that you'd gone to live somewhere else." Distress lined her face as she seemed to grasp for the old memories. But then she smiled, looking up at him again. "So you met Jana at Estelle's?"

"Yeah." He told Maddie about the first time he saw Jana's pugnacious young face. "She had a way of taking my mind off everything that was eating me up inside. She'd tell some ridiculous joke that should only have been funny to a ten-year-old girl, but somehow I'd be laughing with her."

He let the storyteller in him take over, describing the trips to the river to collect tadpoles, the snowball fights up at Lake Tahoe. It occurred to him that during those years, Jana had given him the childhood he'd never had.

Then there was that day when everything changed. When he showed up at Estelle's and Jana, now a willowy twenty, was there showing off the dress she'd borrowed for a date with her latest boyfriend. Seeing her in that electric-blue, strapless cocktail dress had sucked the air right out of his lungs. Yeah, she was still just a friend, but she was a woman, not a little girl anymore. And to be honest, that was the first time he'd wondered about kissing her.

Maddie was studying his face, and damned if she wasn't poking into his mind again. "Just friends, huh?" He saw the laughter in her blue eyes, so close a match to his they were like his own reflection in a mirror.

"I think you're so in love with Matthew you want to see that same passion in everyone else."

She shrugged. "What do you think of her giving up her baby?"

That was another path he didn't really want

to walk down. He hated the idea but knew he couldn't ever breathe a word to Jana about how he felt. Taking a page out of his sister's book, he shrugged. "Her decision."

"True. But has it crossed your mind…" Maddie turned toward him, fixing him with that familiar blue gaze. "Have you thought about having kids?"

Her whiplash-inducing question left him stuttering. "I…ah…yeah, as a matter of fact. I want kids." Not the usual male thing to do, but having kids, a family, had been a distant dream for a long time. But problematic, the way he couldn't keep a woman in his life.

One corner of Maddie's mouth dipped down, and he had a sudden flash of déjà vu, of two-year-old Maddie frowning that way. "You'd have to think long and hard about it. It's not something you'd ever take on lightly. But if she's determined to give up her baby…"

As Maddie verbally danced, prescience

prickled up his spine. "What the hell are you talking about?"

"About Jana's baby." Maddie laid her hand on his arm, the seriousness of her expression sending another wave of foreboding through him. "Why not adopt the baby yourself?"

Chapter Ten

Maddie's bombshell suggestion pretty much knocked the stuffing out of Sam. He, in turn, felt both stupid for not thinking of it himself and completely terrified at the thought. Mixed in that stew of emotions was an unexpected joy that he could have a child of his own. Even better, a child that came from Jana, the one person he cared about most in the world.

Sure, he had no clue about how to be a father—he certainly couldn't emulate his own absent dad, who spent far more time with his job as a long-haul trucker than with his family. And he wasn't certain he could pull off the mothering side of the equation either—except to do it differently than the confused and messed-up mother who deserted him and Maddie.

Amidst all that heavy thought, he completely forgot about his promise to have dinner with Jana that night. It wasn't until two-thirty in the morning, as he stood at his bedroom window, staring out at the darkness, that he recalled his broken commitment.

By then it was too damn late to call and apologize. He wondered why Jana hadn't called him to remind him, then got riled up worried about her, that something had happened to prevent her from reaching the phone. When he still couldn't get that thought out of his mind an hour later, he dressed and drove down to the apartment, parking on the Carson Road side, where her bedroom window faced.

He drifted off a couple of times in the cramped driver's seat, but finally at five-thirty or so, her light came on. He took that as a sign that she was okay and went back home to scrape together a few hours of sleep.

The moment his eyes opened at just past eleven, he called her. When her cell went to voice mail, his sleep-deprived brain crafted a barely coherent message; then he stumbled to the shower.

Now fully awake, he dithered with the phone in his hand. Should he mention Maddie's suggestion? No, bad idea. He hadn't come close to making up his mind. Whether his adoption of Jana's baby would thrill her or chill her, he shouldn't be giving her grief until he was sure. So he'd keep it to himself for now.

He pressed her speed dial key again. This time, she answered.

He didn't even bother with hello. "I'm sorry. I'm a jackass."

Her response was polite and prim and entirely un-Jana-like. "I'm sure you have plenty on your mind."

Good God, did she know? Had Maddie somehow tracked down Jana's cell number and called her, laid out her outrageous suggestion? He shook off the crazy, impossible notion. Jana was probably just ticked off that he'd forgotten dinner.

"Let me make it up to you," he told her. "Come over here for dinner tonight."

"You're going to cook?" Now she sounded like the old Jana.

"A caterer friend owes me one. I'll have her send over dinner."

"Is she one of your kiss-offs?" Now she sounded nasty, even more out of character for Jana than the politeness.

What alien has stolen my good buddy? "I met the caterer and her husband at a chamber of commerce event. Seven o'clock sound okay?"

"I guess. What about lunch? I seem to have an excess of spaghetti and meatballs in my fridge."

"Yeah, I can— No, wait." He checked the calendar on his phone. "Damn. I've got this thing at noon with my agent. I can come over after, maybe around two."

"I have a doctor's appointment. Then I'm meeting with a lady. At that agency." The last three words came out raw, as if dragged from her throat.

About to ask what agency she meant, it hit him like a semi. *The adoption agency.* "You finally made the appointment."

"I thought I better."

Should he tell her now? But he still wasn't sure. What if he got cold feet? If he couldn't commit to a woman, for God's sake, how could he commit to a ten-times-more-needy baby?

The best he could come up with was an offer. "You want me to go with you?"

Silence for five long seconds. "I'd rather do this alone."

Now he felt like a real heel for keeping quiet. But although he could impulsively offer her money, could change his life on a dime to help fix up the apartment for her and give her the job preparing the shop for opening, blurting out, "Hey, why don't *I* just adopt your baby," would be beyond wrong.

"Then I'll see you at seven," he said.

"Okay."

He hung up, wishing he could have reached through the phone and given her a hug. He went into his office and sat at his desk in preparation for the conference call with his agent. God only knew how he'd focus on the negotiations for film rights on his next book. He would have rescheduled if his agent hadn't gone through so much trouble setting this up with the Hollywood producers involved.

So when the phone rang, he did his best to shift

gears, to take his mind off Jana. But she was always there in his mind's eye, the image crystal clear—her looking up at him, her expression serious as she placed her baby in his arms.

Jana's was the last appointment of the day at the adoption agency. It was a Friday on top of that, and the lady Jana talked to must have planned a big weekend, because she seemed in an awfully big rush to get through the preliminary interview. But despite her speediness, the woman managed to work in the same question about a dozen times in as many versions.

Are you sure you want to give your child up for adoption?

Jana nodded yes every time, saying it out loud for extra emphasis. It didn't change the screaming no inside her, but she'd stopped listening to that voice when it couldn't come up with a solution for how she'd manage to raise a baby while working and going to school. When she would barely be able to support herself, let alone pay for a sitter.

After the emotional roller coaster of the adoption agency visit, she would have just as soon stayed home. Eaten a third meal of spaghetti and meatballs. But she had a feeling that if she called and canceled, Sam would be on her doorstep about ten minutes later.

The way he'd insisted on her coming over for dinner had made her kind of suspicious. Maybe he wanted to tell Jana that since he'd gotten in touch with his sister again, he wouldn't be able to spend as much time with her. He'd rather use the time he'd been spending with her to see his sister instead. This could be a kiss-off, sort of like the ones he did with his girlfriends, except without the expensive jewelry.

That lit a campfire in her stomach, a burning pain worse than anything the month of morning sickness had thrown at her. Still, she pulled on jeans and what she thought was her cutest maternity top, a short-sleeve, rose-patterned scoop neck, and headed over to Sam's. She knocked to give him warning, then let herself in when she discovered the door was unlocked.

He was halfway down the stairs as she stepped inside. He wore a black dress shirt, the sleeves rolled up, and black slacks that looked custom-made. Despite the sense of impending doom hanging over her, or maybe because of it, all the longing, wanting, hot desire she'd refused to acknowledge these past few months surged in a sudden ambush. So vulnerable after her visit to the adoption agency, laid low by her fear that Sam was about to show her the door, she had nothing in reserve to contain her reaction.

His hurrying steps slowed as he crossed the room toward her. "How'd it go?" Something flashed in his eyes behind the question, but she couldn't figure it out. Hopefully not pity. She'd be pissed if that was all he had left for her.

"It went," she said, fighting to keep the mess inside her out of her voice. "I've got another appointment in a couple weeks."

She followed him into the dining room, then had the breath knocked out of her when she saw what he'd done. Tall white candles in crystal holders, what had to be his best china and actual silver silverware, a gorgeous arrangement of spring flowers and a white tablecloth, for heaven's sake. She stared at the flickering flames, the coral glads with their fuzzy red centers, and just wanted to start bawling. Because this might not be a diamond tennis bracelet, but it was close.

And competing with the tears, a rush of desire washed over her again, completely turning her brain inside out. It made no sense that in the same moment she wanted to break down and cry, she also wanted to beg him to carry her off to his bedroom and make love to her.

Was it because she was more like her mother than she wanted to think? With good old Mom, every road from gratitude would lead to sex, because she didn't know any other way to say thank-you.

Except in that moment, with Sam looking back at her, that expression on his face asking if it was okay what he'd done, if she liked it, Jana didn't care if she'd turned into a clone of her mother. Because Jana wanted him so desperately, to ease the pain inside her, to express how much she appreciated all he'd done for her. She wanted him because he was Sam, because she loved him so damn much and had forever.

He served the meal, kept warm in the oven. Shrimp scampi and pasta, a Caesar salad and crunchy French bread. Tiramisu for dessert, coffee for him and herbal tea for her. They talked about the shop, the latest merchandise that had arrived that day, the big Easter extravaganza at the ranch tomorrow, the progress on his book. She thought he might ask again about her appointment, but although he asked how it went at the doctor, he avoided the other topic.

They moved to the living-room sofa, Jana stretched out at one end, Sam at the other with his feet on the coffee table. Outside, a spring storm rattled the windows.

Should she ask him about his lunch? Introduce the subject so she could be put out of her misery sooner rather than later? He'd been dancing around something all evening. She'd just as soon get it out into the open.

Then he took a big breath and saved her from asking. "I saw my sister today."

Jana's stomach lurched. "Maddie?"

"Madelena. I'm surprised you remember the name. I know I never talked much about her."

The disaster monkey perched on her shoulder, Jana focused on making polite conversation. "How long since you saw her last?"

"Twenty-three years ago, when she was four. We spoke over the phone about ten years ago, but nothing since then."

"I guess you'll be off with her a bunch," Jana said, trying to be casual. "No biggie. I'm fine on my own."

He stared at her as if she'd grown antlers. "She only flew in for the day. She's already back in San Diego."

The rolling turmoil inside Jana came to a screeching halt. "What? Why?"

He shrugged. "Neither one of us was sure how the reunion would go. So she figured she'd just do a day trip this first time. I didn't tell you before now for the same reason. But when she's able to get away again, she's looking forward to meeting you."

He told her more about Maddie, about how she'd attended University of California at San

Diego for her nursing degree and now worked at a research hospital. Her fiancé, a marine, would be permanently deployed in San Diego after this last tour of duty.

"Maddie suggested I bring you to her wedding."

Still reeling from the revelation that Maddie hadn't replaced her in Sam's affections, Jana stuttered out, "When is it?"

"First weekend in December."

She felt like one of those guys in the old Western movies, tied to four horses to be torn apart. There was the horse that wanted to meet Maddie and the one that feared tying herself even more tightly to Sam. The one who would love to go to Maddie's wedding and the one who thought she'd be better off walking away after the baby's birth. At least until she was on her own two feet, to show Sam she could take care of herself.

"We'll see," she said finally.

A powerful gust of wind slammed rain against the back windows. The trees beyond the pool whipped their branches in a crazy dance.

Sam glanced at his watch. "It's nearly ten."

"I should get going." But she didn't move, exhausted by the emotional ruckus of the past few hours.

"Maybe you should stay over. In the guest room."

Why not? She'd slept there any number of times, back when she house-sat for Sam and more recently, when she'd returned from Oregon. But somehow the decision to stay tonight seemed weightier. More dangerous.

Another bucket of water gushed against the window. She thought about slogging out to the Prius, driving back to town, with the wind shaking the small car on the winding roads, getting even wetter racing up the stairs to her apartment.

"I could stay."

"Good."

The decision made, they lapsed into silence. Sam turned, straightening his legs alongside hers. At one time, that would have been the most innocent of gestures. They would have rubbed each other's feet and cracked jokes over whose socks were the smelliest.

But tonight, there was no grade-school humor. The tension between them was too taut, too loaded. Jana's skin felt hot, too tight. It was hard to breathe.

Sam's gaze fixed on her, the blue of his darkening nearly to black in the dim room. His hand fell on her leg, his fingers dipping under the hem of her jeans, stroking from the top of her ankle sock to her calf. Fire followed in the wake of his touch.

As if she were his mirror image, helpless to resist imitating him, she trailed her fingers under the cuff of his slacks. Her heart hammered in her ears as she touched skin, halfway up his calf, felt the coils of hair against her palm. He shifted his leg so she could push the slacks up, allowing her access to the crease of his knee, the beginning of his muscular thigh.

Her snugger jeans restricted how far he could touch her, leaving her aching, wanting his hands to move higher, along her thigh, to the juncture of her legs. With the loose elastic around the waist, it would be easy enough to slip the jeans from her hips, give him better access. Her head swam with confusion, with flame, as she imagined herself undressing for him.

A tiny piece of common sense floated to the surface, but her throat felt so dry she could barely speak. "What are we doing?" she whispered.

"I don't know. Honestly. I don't have a damn idea."

"We're friends." She swallowed, trying to

work a little moisture in her mouth. "Do friends do stuff like this?"

She hadn't even felt this way with Ian, and he'd supposedly been her lover, her boyfriend. But things had never been this way between her and Sam. Not until the past few months, since she came back from Portland.

And yet she didn't stop touching him, leaning forward slightly to graze the crease behind his knee. His breath caught; she could hear it. He shifted again, and she could see his erection pushing against the fly of his slacks. A movie reel of images spilled from her mind—her unhooking his slacks, slowly lowering the zipper, pushing down slacks and shorts. He wore boxers; she'd seen a pair left on the floor outside his bedroom once.

She could so clearly see how he'd look with his clothes pushed out of the way, the way he'd react if she kissed along that hard length. She'd never liked doing that with Ian, had gone along with it because she thought she should. But she was dying to taste Sam that way.

"Damn it to hell," Sam muttered, shoving off the sofa and striding across the living room. He practically pulled the hair off his head as he paced back and forth across the carpet. Jana couldn't drag her eyes away from him, still fixed on that enticing bulge at his fly.

He caught her looking. Turned his back on her. Managed to make it to the stairs without ever revealing the front of him. Of course that gave her his butt to fantasize about.

He wouldn't have known because he didn't look her way again. "I'm… I've got… Don't think I'll be down again tonight. You know where everything is."

She watched until he disappeared at the top of the stairs. She sat for several more minutes, trying to gather herself. She might as well have been a feather out in that storm, tossed every which way until she didn't know which end was up.

Finally, she levered herself up from the sofa and padded off to the guest room. She thought she'd never fall asleep, but her body took charge and tipped her off into dreamland the moment her head hit the pillow.

Not that he'd really expected to fall asleep when he went upstairs at ten, but he didn't think he'd still be a jittery mess of nerves at two in the morning. The two-hour session at his computer from ten to midnight had only wired him more than Jana's touch had, although he did have a damn good love scene written between Trent and Lacey. Too accurate a description of all the things he'd like to do with Jana, the seven pages would never see the light of day.

When he finally shut down his computer, when he should have had better sense, he'd crept downstairs and to the guest room. When he couldn't hear a sound from within, he'd made another boneheaded move and nudged the slightly ajar door open and cautiously stepped inside. Jana was so dead asleep that she didn't so much as stir as he tiptoed across the floor to stand over her bed.

It reminded him of the story of Cupid and Psyche, except with the gender roles reversed. He was the awestruck mortal, gazing down at the heart-stoppingly beautiful goddess sleeping in his house.

That whimsy had been enough to kick his butt back upstairs. He went through the motions of his nighttime ritual, sliding between the sheets alone when he wanted to be anything but. Then he proceeded to tangle up the bedclothes with tossing and turning when he'd much rather rumple the covers with the sleeping goddess downstairs.

As the digital clock ticked over to two-eleven, he dropped his feet to the floor and pushed out of bed. Maybe a belt of scotch would relax him enough to go to sleep. In his bedroom doorway, he dithered over whether to pull pajama bottoms on over his boxers. But why bother digging them out of his dresser drawer? When he'd checked on her, Jana had looked so lost to the world a herd of Disney hippos in tutus wouldn't have wakened her.

He took the carpeted stairs as quietly as he could, with only the sixth step from the bottom squeaking under his weight, as usual. Certainly not loud enough to reach as far as the guest room.

He was halfway across the living room before the pale glow of a kitchen light registered. Not as bright as the overhead fluorescents—maybe the downspot over the sink. Maybe Jana had left it on before she went to bed. He hadn't noticed it when he'd come down earlier. In fact, he'd bumped a toe on one of the side tables because it had been so dark.

So, if he accepted the concepts of gravity, the sun rising in the east, the Sacramento River Cats being the best Triple-A ball club on the face of the planet, he should acknowledge that the light in the kitchen was on only because Jana was in there and not asleep in the guest room. And he most definitely shouldn't go in there to check, just to be sure.

And yet his feet started moving toward the kitchen, irresistibly drawn to the compulsion that was Jana. All too aware of the cool air on his body, the vast areas of skin the boxers didn't cover. How it might look to go popping into the kitchen nearly naked.

But then he stepped inside and saw her, and he didn't give a damn. She was leaning against the counter by the kitchen sink, a glass of milk cradled in her hands. She wore a worn-out T-shirt, one of his, if he wasn't mistaken. And although the kitchen island blocked his view of her below the waist, he suspected that other than maybe panties, she wasn't wearing anything but the shirt, not if those two little points pressing against the soft knit were any indication.

His erection came on hard and fast, threatening to push itself out of the open fly on the boxers. He stepped up to the island to shield himself, which had the side benefit of giving him a great view of her bare legs from hip to knee.

"What are you doing up?" She gazed at him warily, clutching her glass to her chest, her bent arms framing her breasts.

Stay put! Don't you dare go over there. As extra enforcement, he gripped the smooth granite of the island. "Couldn't sleep. Thought you were down for the count, though."

That was a mistake; he could see it in the

narrowing of her eyes. "How do you know whether or not I was asleep?"

"You seemed tired. Like you'd fall asleep pretty quick." He forked his fingers through his hair, wishing he could reach in and pluck out the randy thoughts dancing through his mind.

"I did. But I heard this big bang. It woke me up. I couldn't fall asleep again, so I thought I'd go for the warm milk."

She took another sip, her eyes drifting shut. His eyes drifted, too, down her body to her breasts, to those faint bumps in the T-shirt that told him where her nipples were. Somehow, he'd moved around the island, closer to her.

Anchoring his ankles in imaginary shackles, he gave himself a mental slap. "Where'd you find the shirt?"

She opened her eyes again. "From that giveaway bag you keep in the coat closet. I figured you wouldn't mind."

"Sure. No problem." Damn, he'd moved

closer again. Now he stood two feet from her, could scan her delicious body from head to toe. Her slightly swollen belly only added to her allure, tempting him to run his hand over it, imagine the baby within.

A baby that could be his. That idea went through him like a bolt of lightning. Should have derailed him from the sex track but somehow instead added coal to the roaring engine.

Her gaze locked with his, she set the glass on the counter, nearly upsetting it. He grabbed for it to set it into place, in the process gathering up her hand, drawing it to his mouth. He pressed a kiss to the back of her fingers, then traced his tongue along the middle one to its tip.

Her soft sigh galvanized him, tugging his attention to her mouth. After that brief kiss at the ranch nearly a month ago, he'd relived it a thousand times, embellished it, extrapolated it. He could follow through on all those fantasies right here, right now.

His lips brushed hers softly at first, just in case she wanted to object. When she leaned in closer, her mouth opening to his, he knew he was going to have to take his own sweet time exploring, tasting. He dipped his tongue inside, groaning at the honeyed warmth, feeling her hum of responding pleasure vibrating against his lips.

As he wrapped his arm around her, her free hand settled on his chest. A part of him, the part that still clung to a microgram of sanity, hoped she'd push him away. But instead, she trailed her fingers through the curls of hair, her nails scudding against his heated flesh. His erection throbbed so powerfully he wondered if he'd lose control right there in his kitchen, shame himself in a way he hadn't since he was eighteen, making out with Melinda Barker in the backseat of her dad's Chrysler.

Damn, her hand was moving lower. Down the center of his torso, to his navel, pausing there to send a shiver through him as she stroked inside. Then he felt her fingertips at the elastic of his shorts. She didn't slide her hand beneath, and regret and relief duked it out inside him. But then she drifted lower, to the gap where the fly opened. In the next explosive instant, she'd worked her fingers inside and wrapped them around him.

He gripped her even harder, turning to lean against the counter to keep his knees from buckling. He reached for her shoulders, tried to push her away, to give his lungs a chance to drag in a little air. But then she was gone as she bent, going to her knees, and took him into her mouth.

He couldn't, he wouldn't let her—he couldn't stop her. Had no strength to pull away from her and the explosion building in his body, the brilliant light and heat and sensation.

That this was Jana pleasuring him, the one person he'd felt more connection to than any other, tipped mind-blowing into miraculous.

Just when he thought he might step away, her hand gently cupped him, stroking as her soft mouth blasted him to infinity. His body arched as the climax hit like a semi from heaven, Jana moaning as if she came, too, just from the contact high. Her tongue licked one last time along his length, imploding his lungs; then she sat back on her heels.

Straightening his boxers, too shell-shocked to put two thoughts together, he stared down at her. Since he blocked the downspot, her face was mostly in shadow and he couldn't quite read what might be going on inside her. But damned if he wasn't ready for round two, except this time turnabout was fair play.

He helped her up, felt her tremble. Didn't like the troubled look on her face. The way she avoided meeting his gaze.

"I…" she glanced at him sidelong, then away "…shouldn't have—"

"Stop." He tried to cupped her chin, make her look at him, but she wriggled away.

"I have to go to bed."

He could hear tears in her voice as she hurried from the kitchen, and he felt like the lowest form of animal. Even lower, like a worm. What the hell was he thinking, traipsing into the kitchen the way he did, knowing she was here? After what had happened on the sofa earlier?

Because this is exactly what you wanted, he told himself and felt even worse. A worm wouldn't even want to keep company with him.

He rushed after her, at a loss as to how to fix what he'd broken. But by the time he'd reached the guest room, she'd already locked herself inside. She wouldn't answer his knock.

After ten minutes of trying, he dragged himself off to bed, skin crawling with remorse. Wishing he could somehow replay the past half hour. And hoping against hope that he hadn't ruined everything with her.

She curled herself up tightly into a ball—at least as tight as she could, considering the cantaloupe-size lump in her belly. She spread her hands over her eyes in a vain effort to block out the memories. The luscious feel of Sam against her mouth, the exhilaration of feeling his climax against her lips.

Her body tightened at just the memory. She'd nearly gone over the edge herself. Just from holding him, touching him.

But how could she? This wasn't the relationship she and Sam had. They were friends, not...what? Lovers? Pleasure pals?

She could only hope, pray that her actions hadn't totally messed up everything with Sam. She didn't even know how she'd face him in the morning. Or tomorrow at the Easter egg hunt. Or ever for the rest of her life.

Stop thinking about how good it felt. She shouldn't have done it. It was a completely brainless move. And she absolutely, positively should not be thinking about how much she wanted to do it again.

Chapter Eleven

Jana crossed the front lawn of the Estelle's House ranch, her sandals squishing a little in the rain-soaked grass, dodging kids from toddler size to middle-graders as they zipped around searching for eggs. Good thing the storm had quit dumping the wet stuff by six, when Jana had crept out of Sam's house. And since the hunt had been scheduled at one, there had been time for the lawn to dry out a bit.

They couldn't have asked for a more

gorgeous day. If Jana wasn't so turned inside out and upside down, that bright blue sky and sweet light breeze that fluttered the full skirt of her maternity dress might have lifted her spirits. But the sky reminded her of Sam's eyes, the puffs of wind of his touch. In fact, everything she'd seen and smelled and tasted today, from the apple fritters the Estelle's House teens had made for breakfast to the dark hot decaf she'd warmed her hands with, reminded her of the explosive fire of last night.

It had been like watching one of the Trent Garner action movies or reading one of Sam's books. Everything happening at once, boom, boom, boom. Never a chance to catch your breath. Never a chance to think and consider just how stupid your actions might be.

Jana paused as Tony and Rebecca's daughter, Lea, and another five-year-old girl dashed madly across Jana's path. They were both screaming with laughter, the eggs in their baskets threatening to bounce right out. What a difference from the sad-eyed Lea that Jana had babysat only last year.

With the coast finally clear, Jana reached the booth for the beanbag toss game and stepped inside. She and Frances would be manning the booth when it opened after the kids finished the egg hunt.

A small commotion caught Jana's eye, and a moment later she heard a kid wailing. A little boy, maybe three, had slipped on the wet grass and dropped his basket of eggs. Sam was right there, asking the kids around him to gather up the little guy's eggs, sending one of the teens for a towel to wipe some of the mud off his bottom. In nothing flat, the three-year-old was giggling up at Sam, his basket a few eggs heavier because the older kids had added one or two of their own.

No doubt because of Sam. She could see even from across the lawn how the kids adored him.

The littlest ones stared up at him in awe, heads cranked way back to see the top of six-foot-four Sam. The middle-graders flocked around him as if he were Harry Potter, Spider-Man and Luke Skywalker all rolled into one. The teen girls were madly in love with him, and the boys all wanted to be like him.

He crouched to give the muddy little guy a hug, his long arms just about able to wrap around the kid twice with some to spare. She couldn't quite make out Sam's face, but the way he held the kid in his embrace, the way he patted his back before letting him loose to run like a maniac across the lawn again, tugged at Jana's insides. She'd never thought about it much, but she realized he'd always been good with kids, had always liked them. Lucky for her or he might have never noticed her at Estelle's all those years ago.

He straightened, his jeans wet from kneeling beside the toddler. Her heart flip-flopped seeing that. He didn't care about messing himself up if it meant comforting a child.

Then he turned to scan the crowd. A prickle danced up and down Jana's spine as she realized he was looking for her. She was half-tempted to dive behind the booth's counter. She could tell Frances she was going through the prizes so she could sort them by color or something equally ridiculous.

But she didn't. She let him find her, felt the prickle turn into a torrent of heat as his gaze locked with hers. She struggled to breathe as he strode purposefully in her direction.

She wasn't ready to talk to him yet. She'd avoided him this morning when she had skipped out early, had conveniently ignored his calls on her cell phone and had arrived here at the last minute when the place was totally cuckoo with the impending egg hunt. Unless Frances turned up quickly or she had a sudden influx of customers at the beanbag toss, it was time to face the music.

He leaned toward her across the counter. "We should talk."

She fidgeted with the skirt of her dress. "Could we just forget it ever happened?"

His gaze grew so hot she thought he might laser-zap her to a crisp. "Not something I'm ever likely to forget. But I don't want you thinking... You damn well shouldn't be blaming yourself for anything." He reached into the booth, took her hand. "Are you?"

"I don't know why I did it, Sam. I mean I do know, except..."

"Except neither of us wants to go there. Right?" His warm hand enfolded hers, his thumb stroking the back of it. For someone who didn't want to go someplace, he was sure laying out the map and drawing the route.

She forced herself to blank her mind to his touch, although her body wasn't going along with it. Sensation rippled up her arm.

She had to work hard to keep the trembling

from her voice when she spoke. "Just tell me we're still friends."

"The best of friends." He took a breath, as if about to add something else. But Frances arrived just then, ducking behind the booth with a wide grin, her lip ring bobbing. Sam let go of Jana's hand, then walked off with a wave.

Jana still felt funny inside about what had happened last night. Partly because she didn't yet know how it was all going to shake out with her and Sam's friendship, partly because her mind kept replaying every sensual moment. To be gospel-truth honest, she wanted to do it again. That and more.

But as the kids started lining up and she put beanbags into small hands, she knew a repeat performance was never going to happen. Never should happen. Because it was pretty obvious that was a direction Sam just didn't want to go. She had to return to her original plan—stay with Sam for the time being, have her baby, move on with her life. Maybe move away from the area again to make a clean break.

It didn't matter that the thought pretty much destroyed her heart. She'd find a way to survive the pain.

He could barely take his eyes off her the whole day. Whether she was lifting up a four-year-old to help her get her beanbags into the frog's mouth or spinning cotton candy at one of the snack stands, his fascination with Jana filled every ounce of his awareness. He'd managed to do a passable job at the goldfish game, sneaking a Ping-Pong ball into a water-filled bowl if it didn't bounce in on its own, keeping the relish and chopped onions filled by the hot dog stand. But more than once, one of Tony's teens had to yell at him to get his attention when he was preoccupied with gawking at Jana.

She was so damn good with the kids. It broke

his heart that she was having to give up the baby. She really ought to be raising it herself.

It was seven by the time the last cranky kid had been bundled into his parents' car and the teens started the cleanup operation. When Rebecca wouldn't let Sam lift a finger to help, he scoped out the grounds to see where Jana had gone. When he didn't see her immediately, his gaze jumped to the parking lot. The Prius was gone.

Rebecca nudged him aside so she could pick up some trash under his foot. "She was beat. She went home."

He considered playing it cool and asking who she meant. But Rebecca wasn't stupid. She'd never go for it. Instead, he asked, "Where's Estelle?"

"In the house. Where I'll be in about five minutes. Ruby's got these kids well in hand."

Ruby had been a student in the first session of the Estelle's House program and was now employed as housemother. "See you in a few, then," Sam said as he walked toward the house.

Tony must have seen him approach through the window because he had the door open before Sam hit the porch. "Come on in. Can I get you a beer?"

"No, thanks." He didn't dare drive the Mustang down the curving foothill roads with a beer in his system. "Estelle in her room?" Estelle shared the downstairs bedroom with Ruby.

"Yeah. Pretty tired, though. I don't think she's up to a long visit."

Anxiety for his former foster mom bubbled in his stomach. "Seems like she's always tired."

Tony made a face. "Whatever her doctor's been telling her, she's not sharing it with me or Rebecca. Just keep it short with her."

Sam nodded in agreement, then headed for the bedroom. He knocked and called out,

"It's Sam," then slipped inside when she invited him in.

One look at Estelle, and his concern for her rose another notch. Propped up in the bed with a book in her lap, she had dark circles under her eyes and her hands and ankles were swollen. She looked years older than the last time he saw her, only a month ago.

He hovered by the door. "I hate to bother you. If you're too tired—"

"Oh, come in, for goodness' sake. That Tony wants to mother me to death."

A chill traveled up his neck at her use of the word, but he moved to sit at the foot of the bed. "I need some advice."

She set aside her book with a smile. "I haven't had the chance to butt into your life in a long time."

With her smile, she looked younger again, the way he remembered her. The knot in his stomach eased. "I've been in contact with my sister, Maddie."

Now she beamed. "That's great."

"It's fantastic. We had a long lunch the other day. I told her about my career, about the ranch program." He took in a long breath. "And about Jana and the baby."

"And?" Estelle prodded.

"Maddie had kind of a crazy idea. Except I haven't been able to think about anything else." Sam met his former foster mother's gaze, so he could be sure to see her reaction. "Maddie thinks maybe I should adopt Jana's baby."

Estelle folded her hands in her lap. "To be honest, Sam, I'd considered the same thing. You certainly have the wherewithal to bring up a child. You're a good man and you'll make a good father."

"But?" She hadn't said it, but he could hear it in her tone.

"But…" She sighed, her gaze falling to her linked, swollen hands a moment before she looked up at him again. "You grew up without a mother." She held up her hand against his protest. "I did my best with you, but I was not your mother. I gave you all the love I could, but we both know how many others there were in the house."

He moved beside her on the bed, took her hand. "I never felt cheated or shorted. None of us did."

"In any case, do you want your own child growing up without a mother? When you have a choice and could choose otherwise?"

He struggled to parse out what she was trying to say to him. "You mean don't adopt the baby? Let someone else, a married couple, take the baby?"

She shook her head. "No, I think you should. But you need to come up with the rest on your own," she finished cryptically. She leaned back in the bed. "Now I do need to rest."

He gave her a gentle hug, then left the room. Too full of his own thoughts, he passed on

Rebecca's offer of dinner and headed out. But instead of turning toward home, he pulled onto the freeway and started up the hill toward Lake Tahoe.

He got as far as Desolation Wilderness, pulling the Mustang into the turnout and climbing from the car. The moonless sky had faded to nearly black, with only the occasional passing headlight providing illumination. The air was chill this high up and dirty snow still lined the sides of Highway 50.

He wanted Jana with him here. Wanted to gaze up at the mountainside with her, listen together to the roar of Horsetail Falls in the distance. To soak up the cool night air, talk about how in the summer, after the baby was born, they'd hike to the top together.

He tried to imagine what it would be like to have Jana hand her baby over to a pair of strangers. It just about killed him. The child was part of Jana and, in a way, a part of him, even though he'd had nothing to do with the creation of it. How could he let the baby pass out of his life?

He couldn't. Even if he would be raising the baby alone, without a mother. Even if—especially if—Jana left again afterward. He'd need the baby then, a reminder of her.

He got behind the wheel again, turning the car around and heading back down the hill. It was past eight—too late to go to Jana's as tired as she'd been? He'd have to play it by ear, check to see if her lights were still on.

He felt ready to burst with anticipation by the time he pulled off the freeway in Camino. He drove down Carson Road, saw her street-facing bedroom light glowing. Parking behind the store, he climbed the steps two at a time, rapped on the door.

He had it all detailed in his mind, how he'd present the adoption idea to her, the arguments she might make against it and how he'd counter them. He rehearsed his opening as he listened for her footsteps, editing it as he would a paragraph in one of his books.

Then the dead bolt clattered and the door swung open. Her fragrance hit him first, the faintest dream of honeysuckle. Then his eyes filled up with pink—her ruffly pink babydolls, the flush on her throat where her pulse beat. And his mind wiped clean, as empty as the day he was born.

He couldn't breathe. Heat exploded in his body from the center out.

"Sam." She whispered his name so softly it was a caress against his skin. An invitation she seconded with her eyes, with her hand reaching across the space between them.

In one motion, he stepped inside, kicking the door shut behind him as he gathered her in his arms. She spread her hands across his chest, sliding them up to lock her fingers behind his neck. The swell of her belly between them filled him with an irrational pride. This would be his child, his baby. He knew it with a dead certainty.

But her mouth eagerly accepting his, her fingers threading through his hair pushed aside that needed conversation. As he kissed her, his hands stroking her through the thin fabric of her babydoll shirt, he backed her down the hall toward the bedroom. She stayed with him each step, her touch as urgent, her mouth as hot as his.

Impatient, mindless, he tugged off her top, tossing it aside. Drinking in the sight of her breasts, still small but rounded with her pregnancy, he bent his head, taking one nipple into his mouth as he stroked the other with his fingers. She gasped, throwing her head back. He felt her knees give way.

He caught her, easing her back onto the bed. Standing over her, he splayed his hand over her belly. "So damn sexy."

She started to shake her head, then he let his fingers drift lower to the elastic waist of her shorts. He watched her eyes widen as he pushed inside, cupping the soft curls at the vee of her legs.

"Incredibly sexy," he murmured as he lowered to kiss her.

While he brushed her lips with his, he explored her folds, the silkiness, the moistness between them. She moaned into his mouth and he drank in the sound.

He stroked her, rubbed her, dipping a finger inside her to feel her slick, wet heat. Reveled in every purr of pleasure, the way her breathing grew rough with passion. As mind-blowing as last night had been, touching her this way, feeling her rise up against his hand, her fingernails digging into his shoulder, was an even greater paradise.

Then she came, her body clenching around his finger, her legs squeezing around his arm so tightly he half wondered if he'd ever pull it free. Then she fell back against the bed, as if every muscle in her body had turned to jelly.

Her eyes drifted open, and he worried that she might be as ashamed of what he'd done as she'd been last night. But then she whispered, "Take off your clothes."

He hoped he wouldn't need his heart, because it had just slammed out of his chest. He stripped off his polo, his jeans and boxers, threw them every which way. Tugged off her dainty pink shorts.

Then he stalled. Kneeling between her legs, still touching her because she felt so damn good, he hesitated.

"What?" she asked, worry beginning to creep into her face.

"I've always used a condom."

Her mouth curved in a beguiling smile. "I think that ship has sailed."

He stroked her belly. "Not the only reason."

"He was my first, Sam. I was his. He was a jerk but not a sleep-around jerk." Her eyes half closed as he found a particularly sensitive spot on her body. "So, if you've been careful…"

He had. Had been tested, declared A-OK. And he could only be so noble as she reached for him, her hands on his hips urging him toward her, into the cradle of her thighs.

With his first stroke inside her, his eyes just about rolled back inside his head. He had to stop, gasp for breath, find a way to balance himself on his elbows to keep from collapsing on her and the baby. Thought he might die in that instant from the pleasure of it.

Then she shifted, pulling him even deeper, her fingers digging into his hips. Her legs wrapped around him, ankles locking at the small of his back. The moan low in her throat, her musky smell, the feel of her breath on his cheek scraped every nerve raw.

Then he started to move, pulling out, then thrusting in, forcing a slow rhythm, battling for control. Even as she squirmed against him, reaching for her own climax, he fought to hold off, wanting every exquisite moment to last, not ready to give in to his body's imperative.

Then she came, jolting, hips thrust up against him, her body vibrating with pleasure. His own body took over, shoving him abruptly into his climax, tossing him into a formless space filled with sensation. Jana was his only anchor, his path back to earth. He clung to her as bit by bit he returned to himself. As bit by bit, the reality of what they'd just done crashed in on him.

He kept his face buried in her throat, inhaling honeysuckle, terrified to look at her, see her expression. Where had he just taken their friendship? Had he blasted it to hell with his compulsion to have her? Could they crawl back up this cliff, get back on solid ground again?

He eased back from her, just enough to shift to the mattress and release her from his weight. Kept his eyes shut as he steeled himself for whatever might have changed. This was different from last night because he'd started it, he'd been running things from beginning to end. They could have considered last night an aberration, but not after tonight.

He'd dived too deep. He'd plunged so far inside her—not physically, but emotionally—that their relationship was beginning to feel different. More like what he'd felt with Faith, with Shawna and Cyndy.

Except so far beyond what he'd experienced with them, it might as well be in a different dimension, a different universe. And that shot hot lead through him, a familiar irrational fear he could no more hold back than he could have held back his climax moments ago.

"Sam?"

He hated the anxiety he heard in her voice, hated himself even more for putting it there. He damn well better be man enough to face her and see if there was a hope of backing away from this brink.

He lifted his gaze to her face. And with a shock, realized things were even worse than he'd thought. It was written, clear as day, in her eyes.

But maybe he was mistaken. Maybe that glow, that smile, didn't mean what he thought it did.

Then she took a breath and foreboding crept up his spine. He would have covered her mouth if he could to keep her from saying the words.

She propped herself up with her elbow, tipped her chin up, defiant. And said it, even plainer and stronger than Faith or Shawna ever had.

"I love you, Sam." And just in case it

wasn't clear enough, she added, "As more than a friend. As a lover. As a partner. I love you."

Just like that, the bottom dropped out of his world.

Chapter Twelve

To his credit, he didn't jump up and run out the door like she expected. He just lay there, staring at her, that snakebit look on his face. His hand still lightly stroking her belly, making her ache for another taste of his lovemaking.

She'd known it was a calculated risk coming clean that way. She hadn't even realized she was going to do it until those moments after she'd climaxed the second time. It had been too gigantic to hold inside her, too perfectly beautiful to keep to herself. Even though she might lose everything with those three simple words.

Her heart thundering in her ears, she waited for disaster to catch up with her. Called up every bit of strength in her body to keep her eyes on him, kind of daring him to deny what she'd said. But still he didn't speak. He just had that someone-ran-over-my-dog look in his eyes, so much pain she wondered how he could bear it.

Then he half sat up and she thought, *This is it: he's going.* But he only reached across her for the light, switching it off, plunging them into darkness. No moon outside, the street-lights blocked by her blinds—now they couldn't see each other at all as he settled back beside her.

Then she figured it out. That was exactly why he turned off the lights. So he wouldn't have to look at her. See whatever was in her face that she just couldn't hide anymore.

But he stayed. Gathered her up in his arms, pulled the covers up over them. Spread his hand across her belly as if to lay claim to what was inside. She puzzled over that. Not for long because even though it was barely ten, the long day overcame her. With Sam so close, she could inhale his scent with each breath. His warm body a comfort, she fell asleep.

He stayed all night. When she got up at midnight to pee, she could see the glitter of his open eyes in the faintest bit of light seeping in from outside. And when she woke closer to morning, she could still feel him beside her, although he wasn't holding her anymore.

When she jolted awake at six-thirty, he was gone. Fumbling as she put on her babydolls, she raced out to the living room, catching her toe on a side table when her belly made her clumsy. She said a few words her baby shouldn't hear, then pushed aside the front curtains to look.

His Mustang was still there. It didn't look as if he was behind the wheel. Was he downstairs? She couldn't let him leave, not without talking to him, figuring out what was happening next.

She dressed in about nine seconds, throwing a T-shirt and jeans over her babydolls. Her feet stuffed into fluffy yellow-duck slippers, a silly thrift store purchase she'd made right after Ian had left, she raced down the stairs. The shop door was unlocked, so he had to be here. She took a breath, pulled the door open and stepped inside.

Sam was over by the summer display she'd set up in the window. She'd filled the shelves with colorful teddy bears in sunglasses and whimsical resin animal figures reclining on tiny chaise longues. To one side were outdoor flags with smiling suns, gorgeous flowers and sailboats on the water, their wooden poles poked in a sand-filled lime-green bucket. A

Day-Glo pink bucket on the other side held garden art—butterflies, frogs and dragonflies on metal rods.

He turned as she walked quietly toward him. "You've done a great job here."

"The kids have helped."

He scanned the rest of the shop, much of it still in disarray. She'd focused on the front window so people would get a hint of what the shop was about. "Will it be ready to open in two weeks?" he asked.

"No worries. All the stock is here. Just a couple more shelves to assemble."

Now he faced her, hands shoved into his pockets. "What happened last night... That wasn't my intent."

"It's okay."

He shook his head slowly. "I think we've been letting our relationship go in directions that we...that we probably shouldn't."

A fist squeezed her heart. "Okay." She kept

using that word, even though things were a million miles from being okay.

His face got so serious she thought, *This is it. He's gone from me forever now.* Then he reached for her hand.

"I've got something important to say to you. I want you to think about it, give it some real consideration before you make a decision. It's what I'd planned to talk to you about before we…"

She had no idea where he was going, but she had a feeling she wasn't going to like it. She just nodded, her free arm around her middle, wishing she had some real armor to wrap herself with.

It wouldn't have helped. Because what he said next hit her like a sucker punch from left field.

"I want to adopt your baby."

She hitched in a breath. "Where did that come from?"

"My sister first." Jana pushed down the

pain she felt at the mention of his sister, the reminder that he had someone new in his life who probably meant way more to him than she did. "Then Estelle," Sam continued. "When I asked her for advice yesterday. She'd considered suggesting it herself."

It was wrong to feel betrayed by Estelle, the woman who was more mother to her than her own mom. She didn't even understand why the thought of Sam taking her baby hurt so much.

Because he wants your baby but not you. She couldn't forget his rejection last night of her declaration of love.

"But, Jana, this was building up in my subconscious even before Maddie said anything. Every time I'd think about your baby, about seeing him sent off to strangers, of never seeing him again—"

"It might be a *her,* damn it!" The defense, made ragged by tears, made no sense. But she was grasping for one thing she could control, even if her baby's gender wasn't even it.

He kept going. "Or her. Either way, my heart would break thinking about it. Not only that I would never see the baby, but that you wouldn't either. Because you could be in his…her life. Visit whenever you wanted."

Talk about half a loaf. Maybe it was just the moldy, weevily heel. Because there would be this baby she adored, this man who she loved with every fragment of her being, and she was just a visitor.

But it was far more than she would have otherwise. The woman at the adoption agency was talking about a couple in Boise, another one in Arizona. There was no telling if either one would be willing to have an open adoption.

He took a step toward her. She retreated. "Don't. Please. I can't think if you're too close."

"You don't have to decide now. You've got four more months."

Except how could she possibly turn him down? When she knew he'd give her baby a fabulous life, would be a wonderful father?

She breathed against the rock weighting her chest, fixed him with her gaze. Before she could decide about the baby, they had another little matter to clear up. "What about last night?"

She'd never before seen a man turn beet-red like that. "It was…"

"Incredible." She narrowed her gaze, daring him to contradict her.

"Yeah. Beyond that." He swiped his hands over his face. "You know about me and women, Jana, when they get too close. I care about you so much. I don't want you ending up like them."

"Then just don't. Why does my loving you have to mean you're gonna throw me away?"

Outrage lit his face. "I wouldn't do that! Send you away. But you have to know… I can't love you that way. And the fact that you think you do—"

"Know, not think."

Now he stared her down. "It means I want to run about a hundred miles in the other direction. That I want to give you a wad of cash and set you up down in Sacramento to get some distance. And I don't want to lose you that way."

She shook her head, struggling to understand. "This makes no sense, Sam."

He paced off toward the cashier's counter and settled on the stool behind it. "It doesn't. I know. It's completely irrational. But if you felt what's going on inside me…it's stark terror, Jana. Complete panic. I'm holding it in. Not letting you see the worst of it. But it's taking everything in me not to jump in my car and take off for Texas."

Now she saw it, the tension around his mouth, how stiffly he sat on the stool. All the times she'd poked fun at him about his love-'em-and-leave-'em ways, she'd never known that the whole commitment thing was such a freaking big deal for him.

And she'd pushed his panic button.

Barely able to hold her own self together, she walked slowly toward him. "I need some time to think about this. About your offer to adopt."

He gave her a brusque nod. "Of course."

She moved to the other side of the register from him, putting the waist-high counter between them. "I've been going one way in my mind about the baby. I've gotta readjust."

Another nod. He looked miserable, as if a fire was burning him from the inside out.

"Sam," she said quietly. "I wonder…maybe if you told me about what happened when you were a kid—"

"No."

"I know your mom left you. Your dad died. Your sister got adopted, but you ended up in foster care—"

"Not open to discussion," he snapped.

"But you gotta know it's all connected," she persisted. "Whatever happened—"

"Damn it, Jana, drop it!"

Now he shoved back from the stool so hard it fell backward. He dragged his fingers through his hair as he paced.

"Rehashing old history won't make a damn bit of difference. It's not like it'll pass a magic wand over me and suddenly I'll love you!"

Jana gasped in pain, all the air leaving her lungs. Shaking all over, she backed away from him and turned toward the back door. He shouted her name, grabbed her arm when he caught up. "I'm sorry. I'm the world's biggest jerk."

She let her tears fall. "You can't stop me from loving you, Sam Harrison. So you'll just have to deal with it."

She tore away from him, running up the stairs. She got to the top well before him. If he came after her, she wasn't about to let him in.

But as she leaned against the locked door, his footsteps stopped halfway up. There was a long pause; then she heard him descend again. Moments later, the back door to the shop slammed shut; sometime after that, the Mustang's engine roared to life.

Feeling desolate, she wandered into her bedroom and tugged open the top drawer of the little dresser Sam had bought her. She'd hidden Sam's letters under the underwear when she'd first moved in and hadn't looked at them since.

She pulled them out now, slipping each one from its envelope, reading them all, from the short, one-paragraph notes to the two- and three-pagers.

Her love for him spilled out as she read each precious word. And she realized there was no better person to raise her child than the one she loved so dearly.

The following Sunday, on Easter, after she'd

spent an exhausting, draining week getting the shop ready for opening, she called him. She didn't bother with hello.

"You can adopt my baby, Sam. Just tell me what I need to do."

She hung up after about thirty seconds of awkward conversation, went into her bedroom and sobbed into her pillow for the next hour.

By opening day the following Saturday, Sam had Darius tracking down Ian Wilson. His attorney was drawing up the adoption papers and he'd figured out about a hundred million ways to call himself a coldhearted jackass. On the plus side, his book was going great, his female foil, Lacey, giving Trent hell, a literary expiation of Sam's personal sins.

Because Celebration Station's profits would be benefiting the Estelle's House independent living program, Sam's publisher had donated fifty hardback copies of his most recent book to be used as giveaways. Sam's publicist had sent press releases to the *Mountain Democrat* in Placerville and the *Sacramento Bee* stating that the first fifty customers would receive a free autographed book. Sam wasn't sure if they'd reach fifty customers for the entire weekend but figured it was worth a try.

The books were gone in the first two hours on Saturday. True, some of the happy fans made a beeline to Sam's table, tucked in a back corner, and left just as quickly with only the book in hand. But at least half of the fifty lingered in the store to browse the flamboyant spring whirligigs, the gorgeous silk flowers for Mother's Day and the patriotic Memorial Day banners. Several of the shoppers had walked out with their arms full of the clever and sometimes wacky seasonal decorations Jana had filled Celebration Station with.

Since Sam was done signing at noon, he

offered to pitch in. Jana sent him out for lunch, then tasked him to handle the press when they arrived. Two of the local network affiliates actually sent news vans to cover the opening. Not only were both the local newspapers eager for interviews, but the *San Francisco Chronicle* had tapped a stringer to drive up to the foothills. Sam spent the entire afternoon yakking with them, doing stand-up interviews with the TV people, grinning like an idiot in front of the store while the photographers filled their digital camera memory sticks.

Every time he tried to bring Jana into the conversation—damn it all, she was the one who'd done ninety percent of the work—she waved him off. Too busy, too tired, too preoccupied. Too pissed at him was more like it. And too hurt, too terribly wounded by what he'd said.

Finally, when the newspeople had scampered off to file their stories, when Ray and Frances had ushered the last customer out the door and then left themselves, Sam thought he might finally have a chance to talk with Jana. Except that when he crossed the store to where she was ringing out the register, she looked tempted to bolt.

But she stood her ground. "We're completely out of the garden art. There's one dragonfly left, but one of its wings is broken. I just about had to put a lady into a half nelson to keep her from buying it. Had to promise I'd save her one from the next shipment."

She took a breath, as if to launch into another recitation. He put up a hand to stop her. "Can we get another shipment by tomorrow?"

"We'd have to pay extra to bring them in from a warehouse in Reno."

"Go ahead and call. Use the AmEx card. Anything else we'll be short on tomorrow?"

She pushed a sheet of paper over. "Same warehouse has most of these."

"Get what you can. The rest will just have to

be on order." He glanced out the front window as a logging truck moved slowly down Carson. "How long before you're done?"

"Another ten minutes. Ray and Frances will be here early to help with setup."

The two teens had arranged with Tony to use work in the shop as their training, rather than the kitchen work that Rebecca taught. They were both taking online business classes with the nearby junior college. Celebration Station fit better with their future plans.

"I'm taking you out to dinner." He put enough emphasis in the words to make sure she understood he wasn't taking any arguments. "I'm going to run home to change, then be back in thirty to pick you up."

She shrugged, then nodded. He headed out, half tempted to demand the car keys to the Prius so she couldn't escape. But she'd agreed. He'd have to trust her. Which, of course, was not one of his strong suits.

But she was there when he climbed the stairs to her apartment a half hour later. When she opened the door, wearing the same flowing flowered dress she'd worn at the Easter egg hunt, honeysuckle teasing his nose, he was a heartbeat away from backing her into the apartment as he'd done two weeks before. Maybe she saw it in his face, because she quickly stepped past him onto the landing, then down the stairs.

Damn, he had to get a grip. It didn't help that her scent drifted across the small space of the DeLorean. Or that he could see the shadow of her cleavage down the front of her scoop-neck bodice. He stole a quick glance before he put the blinkers on and just drove, but it was enough to start the inner X-rated newsreel.

He turned the car over to an ecstatic attendant at the Sequoia in Placerville, then, with his hand on the small of Jana's back, he escorted her into the upscale restaurant. The maître d' seated him and Jana at a table so secluded he'd need a trail of bread crumbs to find his way back to the front door. As packed as the popular restaurant was, their back table could have been in a private room. But that was exactly what he'd asked for when he'd made his reservation.

He ordered a beer; she asked for cranberry juice. They left their menus closed on the table.

Once the drinks arrived, he figured his moment of truth had, too. "Whatever you want to know about me, I'll tell you."

Sipping her juice, she lifted her gaze to his. He saw the wary surprise give way to determination.

"Tell me about your mother."

He should have expected Jana wouldn't pull any punches. But he might as well get the worst of it out of the way first.

He took a swallow of beer. "She had problems. She didn't like that Dad was a long-haul trucker. He wasn't when they married. He just sprang it on her one day a couple months after I was born."

"So he was away a lot."

He could almost hear tucked away in the back of Jana's mind, *At least you had a father.* Her dad had walked out before Jana was born, kind of like Ian had skipped on her.

"Gone a couple weeks, back a few days, then gone again. Part of the reason it took so long for my sister to come along. Dad just wasn't around to make another baby."

He'd never understood that about his father. He was pretty closemouthed when he was home, as if he just didn't know what to say to his pretty young wife. He was fifteen years older than her, thirty-six to his wife's twenty-one when they'd married.

Almost like him and Jana. That was a kick in the teeth.

"I think there was more to it than Mom

just missing Dad. Knowing what I know now, I'm guessing she was depressed. She tried self-medicating with alcohol at first. Moved on to weed, coke. After a while she was buying any kind of crap she could get off the street."

His stomach roiled at the memories. His mother coming home high on God knew what. Needle marks on her arms, which she'd cover with long sleeves even in the summer.

"I think she'd worked her way up to heroin. Don't really know."

"Your father had to have known something was wrong."

"Sometimes they would argue in their bedroom. She'd be in tears, promising things would be different." He shook his head. "Then Dad would head out on another long haul, and it was as if the promise had never been made."

Jana reached across the table and took his hand. "What happened when she left?"

This was where it got ugly. The rest of the story, so to speak, that he'd told no one. Only Aunt Barbara knew the truth, and she'd cut him out of her life long ago.

Still, he'd promised Jana he'd tell her anything. He at least kept his commitments. "It was four days before Christmas. I was ten, Maddie two. Mom hadn't bothered with a tree or decorations. Too caught up in her own private escape."

He saw the flicker of understanding in Jana's eyes. His obsession with Christmas probably made sense to her now.

"She went out that night like she did plenty of times. Except this time, she wasn't back by morning. When she wasn't back by nightfall, I was scared spitless."

Maddie kept crying for her mommy, growing fussier by the hour. By the middle of the second day, she wouldn't eat, and that really scared Sam.

"Wasn't there anyone you could call?" Jana asked.

"My dad's sister. Aunt Barbara. The one who—"

"Adopted Maddie." He'd told her that much of the story. "So did you call her?"

"Couldn't get hold of her at first. Then I left a message with my thirteen-year-old cousin. Not the most reliable kid."

She folded his large hand in both of hers. "I've never understood—why did she adopt Maddie, but not you?"

Here was the worst of the story. The part Maddie didn't remember.

His jaw cramped with tension as he pushed the words out. "Because I nearly killed my sister."

Chapter Thirteen

Sam could see Jana try to wrap her mind around his bald statement. Maybe she was thinking he was exaggerating. But even if he could hide the bone-deep guilt in his eyes, he wasn't about to. She wanted to know; he was telling her.

He'd already passed judgment on himself twenty-five years ago. Surely Jana's condemnation couldn't be any worse.

But this was Jana, the most fair-minded

person he knew. Not Aunt Barbara, who'd thought the worst of him from the get-go.

Jana's tone was neutral, gentle, as she asked, "What happened?"

He let the silence stretch a few more moments as he took another pull of his beer. Then he continued. "By Christmas Eve morning, I figured out why my sister was so cranky and wouldn't eat. She was burning up with fever. She started getting kind of glassy-eyed and after a while she wasn't even crying anymore."

It was like a knife in his chest remembering that listless little girl. She'd always been so cheerful, such a happy baby. Seeing her like that had been painful beyond bearing.

"I knew enough not to give her the grown-up medicine, but I couldn't find the baby aspirin. She kept getting sicker. I called Aunt Barbara again, but she must have gone out to dinner for Christmas Eve. I should have called

911, should have gone to a neighbor, but I just wasn't thinking clearly."

The waiter hovered nearby; Jana waved him off with a dark look. Sam shut his eyes, just letting the memories resurrect themselves, his voice foreign to his own ears.

"I'd seen my mother put Maddie in a cool bath once when she had a fever. So I ran a little water in the tub. Just a couple of inches. Not too much because Maddie was so small."

Now it felt as if he was talking about something that had happened to someone else, a movie or a scene in one of his books. How Maddie had cried as he swished the water on her, how her temperature seemed to spike even higher. How he'd left her sitting up in the tub while he raced to his parents' bedroom, thinking maybe the aspirin was in there.

"I was about to go back to the bathroom when someone knocked. I heard Aunt Barbara yelling through the door and ran to answer it.

I guess my cousin finally remembered to give her the message."

He sucked in air. "She asked where Maddie was. When I told her, she pushed past me. Yelled at me for leaving her alone. By the time we got back to the bathroom—"

The rest of it spilled out. Maddie had tried to climb out of the tub, had slipped and hit her head. She'd landed facedown in the water.

Jana's warm hand on his brought him back to the busy restaurant. "How long was she under?"

"I don't know. Aunt Barbara got her out, squeezed the water from her lungs. Maddie started coughing. Aunt Barbara screamed at me. *'You could have killed your sister! You stupid boy!'*"

"But she was okay."

"But she could have died." He pulled his hand free, scrubbed at his face. Wished he could wipe away the images, still sharp after two and a half decades. "If Aunt Barbara had been a few minutes later, Maddie might have been dead."

Jana stared at Sam, wondering how she could pull him out of his self-imposed hell. "You were ten years old."

"I should have known better."

Jana resisted the urge to reach across the table and shake him. "How could you have?"

He sighed, sliding his beer bottle back and forth across the table. "All those years I avoided contacting my sister, I told myself it was pride—if she and Aunt Barbara didn't want me, I didn't want them either. But to be honest, I was terrified that when I talked to Maddie, when I saw her again, I'd see some lasting effect. Brain damage or something."

"But you didn't."

He smiled. "She's smart and funny and kind. I never should have wasted all those years."

The waiter looked their way again. Sam picked up his menu and Jana followed suit. She picked the least expensive item. Sam zeroed in on something as quickly as she did, and the waiter hurried over to take their order.

Jana got back to business as soon as the waiter left. "That can't be why your aunt Barbara sent you away."

He shook his head. "The first two years after my mom left, Dad left us with Aunt Barbara when he was on a haul. I was incorrigible. Lying, stealing from her. Flunking out at school. Then Dad had his wreck. With my dad dead, my behavior got even worse."

"Geez, Sam, you were hurting. I think your aunt could have cut you some slack. Got you some counseling."

"She tried. I wouldn't talk to the counselor. After a while I think she was afraid of me. Afraid of my influence on her own son. Afraid of leaving me alone with Maddie."

Jana could hear the shame in his voice. "I think she started wondering if what happened in the bathtub really was an accident."

That ticked Jana off so much she would have clocked his aunt if the woman had been there. The Sam she knew—a little cocky, way brilliant—was a good man, just about the best person on the planet. How could his aunt have suspected him of trying to hurt his sister?

She reached for his hand again. "So your mom left. Your dad died. Aunt Barbara threw you into foster care and wouldn't let you see your sister. I'm guessing you went through a few foster homes before you found Estelle." He nodded in acknowledgment. "And you were hell on wheels with Estelle at first. She told me that much."

"I did my best to get her to throw me out, too."

"Trying for some control in your life, I guess. Which is what you do every time you buy one of those parting gifts."

"It isn't conscious, Jana. What I feel inside. I don't do it on purpose." She could hear the desperation in his voice. "I've got demons inside me. Pulling me two ways. I'm terrified of losing you. But I'm even more afraid of letting you in."

"But why?"

"Because you won't stay. Either you'll walk away—"

"Not gonna happen."

"—or I will." The lines of his face grew even more tense. "I don't trust myself to not walk out on you. Just like my mother did."

She felt as if she were on a merry-go-round, with Sam as the brass ring. But he kept backing away every time she tried to reach for him.

The waiter brought their salads, a pretty mix of greens and tomatoes that Jana was sure she wouldn't be able to eat. Still, she picked up her fork and poked around among the arugula. "So what now?" she asked.

He pulled a slice of bread from the basket. "We can't sleep with each other anymore."

Of course they couldn't. That would only finish the job of destroying her heart. Then a sudden thought filled her with panic. "What about the baby?"

His gaze swung up to meet hers. "I still want to adopt."

"But will you love the baby? Are you going to let the baby love you?"

She could see from the look on his face that she'd caught him off guard. That he hadn't thought it through. He turned away from her, staring out at the busy restaurant, and she had to fight to keep the tumult inside her at bay.

Then he turned back toward her. "Lots of fathers wonder if they'll love their baby. And they know going in that someday their kid will leave them. Your baby will never, ever feel unloved. Unwanted. Not one day, not one minute. I promise you that."

There was more steel in his voice than a New York City high-rise. Her doubt and fear faded.

They focused on their food then, making their way through the salads and bread, then the entrée when it arrived. Her body had its own idea about whether she should eat, commandeering her through the plate of pasta primavera. Just to give herself some stalling time, she asked for the dessert menu even though she knew she couldn't manage it. Because she knew she wouldn't have a receptive audience for what she was going to suggest.

She gave the menu a cursory look, dreaming briefly of chocolate lava cake, then set it aside. And crossed her fingers. "I think you should talk to your aunt Barbara. And maybe find out what happened to your mother."

He puffed up like a grizzly bear, looking ready to growl. She didn't back down. "You don't have to become her new best friend, eat dinner with her every Sunday night. But for your sake, isn't it time you cleared the air?"

"Maddie made the same suggestion. About finding our mother." He shrugged. "She had a pretty common name. Makes someone much harder to locate, according to Darius. Maybe I'll ask him when we hear back about Ian."

Jana understood enough about Sam to know that much of a concession was huge. Even so, she prodded him. "What about Aunt Barbara? Is she still in the area?"

"According to Maddie. It was Aunt Barbara's car Maddie borrowed to drive up to Placerville for lunch that day." When Jana kept staring at him, he threw up his hands. "Fine. I'll think about calling her. Satisfied?"

Not until you love me, she thought. But it looked as if that was a complete lost cause.

April wore on into May, Sam plunging deep into writing his book to keep the craziness inside him tamped down. Although it should have been a healing process to reveal all to Jana—at least that's what a shrink would have told him—it seemed as if it had stirred up more than it settled. Nightmares he hadn't had in twenty years returned, him running through his old house, searching for Maddie, finally finding her blue-faced dead. Aunt Barbara screeching at him, the guilt and remorse crushing him.

He couldn't stay away from Jana entirely; it just wasn't in him. He'd share lunch with her and the kids, and they'd go over to the ranch for dinner two or three nights a week. After dinner he'd walk her up to her apartment, give her a chaste hug, then drive home with fantasies running through his head he knew he could never act on.

The third week of May, Sam got the word from Darius that he'd tracked down Ian. The feckless kid had jumped at the chance to sign the termination of parental rights papers. When Sam told Jana, she got quiet, and he wondered if she'd had second thoughts about Ian. Then he realized it was just that it meant the adoption was moving another step forward.

The next week, right before Memorial Day, Maddie got a few days free between shifts and Sam flew her up to Sacramento. The first two nights she stayed with him. He and Maddie and Jana did the touristy thing, heading up to Tahoe one day, the next doing a wine-tasting circuit in Fairplay, with Jana as designated driver.

Maddie and Jana clicked immediately, the way women so often seemed to, joking and teasing, usually at Sam's expense. Maddie tiptoed around the sensitive topic of Jana's baby, asking general questions, readily accepting Jana's offer to feel the baby kick.

That was the only time he let himself touch Jana for more than a few seconds, resting his hand on her belly, waiting for the nudge and bump of that tiny being that would soon be his son or daughter. That first strong kick shot through him like an emotional rocket, leaving him shaken and awed.

Maddie's last night in Northern California she'd promised to spend with Aunt Barbara. And Sam had told his sister he'd give her a lift to her adoptive mom's Roseville home. If he thought he'd have a chance to simply leave Maddie off at the curb, Jana disabused him of that notion pretty quickly. She'd come with him for moral support, but by God he was going to see his aunt Barbara.

He did his best to delay the inevitable. He suggested they stop at a coffee shop in Placerville for waffles and pancakes, then paid the price when the heavy meal sat like a stone in his stomach. After breakfast he took his time putting the top down on the Mustang so they could enjoy the warm late-spring sunshine.

He took the back roads down the hill to Rose-ville, telling the two women there'd be too much wind at freeway speeds.

When they pulled up to the house, Sam felt as if the skin had been stripped from his body. He was that twelve-year-old boy again, defiant and needy, a heartbroken juvenile delinquent. She'd sent him out with two suitcases filled with his stuff; within a year those possessions had been winnowed down to what he could fit in two paper market bags.

Jana smiled at him across the car. Her hair was a riotous mess from riding in the con-vertible, and he wanted to smooth it back into place. He'd want to kiss her after that, despite his sister in the backseat and Aunt Barbara watching from the front window—he'd seen the curtain twitch aside. He'd keep his hands off Jana's hair, but in his imagination, there was a golden link between them that would feed him strength during the upcoming confrontation.

Sam climbed out and retrieved Maddie's suitcase from the trunk. With the two women leading, he carried Maddie's baggage—and a fair load of his own—up the walk. Aunt Barbara had the door open before they got to the stoop.

Damn, she was old. Yeah, it had been more than twenty years and she was close to sixty. But he'd had that midthirties face locked in his mind, that last scowl of disapproval she'd directed his way when she'd delivered him to Child Protective Services.

Her hair might be salt-and-pepper and her face creased with wrinkles, but the scowl was still there. It dropped for a few moments while Maddie introduced Jana as Sam's friend; then it fell back into place. After Maddie and Jana were inside, Aunt Barbara stared at him as if he were the same young miscreant she'd banished from her home twenty-three years ago.

It damn well shouldn't hurt. What did he care what this woman thought of him after all these years? He was a grown man, a big success. Control of his life wasn't in this old woman's hands anymore.

"I'd like to put this down," he said, indicating the suitcase.

She finally stepped aside. He entered, took in the changes of two decades. Updated carpet, furniture. A bookcase full of books he'd bet every penny of his fortune didn't include even one Sam Harrison thriller.

Suitcase set down, an array of family photos caught his attention. He crossed the living room to view them—the school pictures featuring Maddie and his cousin Jason, several with Aunt Barbara, all smiles, with her husband and the two kids. There was one photo of his dad holding baby Maddie, just home from the hospital. Sam remembered that picture used to hang in his parents' bedroom, except he'd been in the photo, too, at his father's side.

No room for Sam Harrison on the bookshelf, no space for him on the wall. Obliterated from Aunt Barbara's life.

She crossed her arms around her stout body. "You've done well for yourself." She said it as if there was something disreputable about his success.

"I've been fortunate."

Jana stepped up beside him. "He's got copies of his latest release in the car." She tugged at his arm, bobbing her head between him and Aunt Barbara.

"I'm glad to give you one." He almost choked on the offer.

Interest flickered in her eyes, just a moment before it was extinguished. "I don't read those kind of books."

He felt Jana stiffen beside him, saw his sister's sympathetic expression. He didn't care what Aunt Barbara might think—he put his arm around Jana. He needed her to hold on to.

Aunt Barbara's gaze slid to Jana's seven-months-pregnant belly. Sam set a proprietary hand there. "Jana is carrying my baby."

He heard Jana's hissing intake of breath. She shot him a glance that he ignored. He directed all his attention toward Aunt Barbara.

"I apologize for being a jackass when I lived here. I was a messed-up kid, and I took it out on you. But everything I am, everything I have, is in spite of what you did to me. And I'm damn well not going to hate you anymore. You're not worth the space in my heart."

He let go of Jana to give his sister a hug. "Let me know when you can come up again." Then he took Jana's hand and started toward the door.

"You look like her," Aunt Barbara called out. "Like your mother."

A rush of cold, then heat, filled Sam. He turned back to his aunt.

"It wasn't because of your behavior," she

said, the lines in her face sharpening. "You were a rotten kid sometimes, but I mostly had you under control."

"Then why?"

Although she did her damnedest, she couldn't quite hide her shame. "Because I saw your mother's face in yours every day. I despised her."

"I've done my share of hating her myself," Sam said.

Her gaze narrowed as her face turned meaner. "She told me you were his. And she refused to get rid of it."

Sam swayed a little as he tried to grasp what his aunt was telling him. "She was pregnant with me when they married?"

"My brother said he believed her, but she didn't fool me. I knew she slept around."

Rage bubbled up inside him. "What are you saying?"

"You know what I'm talking about." She

flicked a dismissive glance at Jana. "You'd better do a paternity test with this one. She looks like the type that would lie to suit herself."

Sam heard a roaring in his ears. He was only dimly aware of Jana clinging to his arm, Maddie moving in to stand between him and Aunt Barbara. It had never in his life even once crossed his mind to strike a woman, but every atom in his body was goading him to break that sacrosanct rule.

But with Jana's fingers digging into his arm, her full weight anchoring him to the floor, he came to his senses. He let Jana drag him out the door and down the walk.

At the sidewalk he shook her off. "I'm okay." Pressing both hands on the hood of the car, he dragged in breath after breath, willing away the nastiness of the scene they'd just left. Jana's gentle hand on his back soothed him, brought him round again.

He took her in his arms, and he could feel her

vibrating with indignation. "What a horrible, despicable, low-life—"

"Do you think it's true?"

She pressed her palm against his face. "Does it matter?"

"Yes. No." He tried to reach inside himself for an answer. "I don't know."

She gazed up at him, her expression earnest. "Does it change the way you feel about your father?"

Now he could hear the real reason for her question. Would he feel differently about the child Jana carried, knowing he or she wasn't biologically his?

"My father was distant. Not cold, but— always awkward with me. But to tell you the truth, he seemed that way with Maddie, too." He allowed himself to kiss Jana's forehead. "Still, I loved him. And in his way, I think he loved me, too. He tried his best."

He opened the car door for Jana and helped

her swing down into the low-slung Mustang. About to round the front of the convertible, he heard Maddie calling him from the house.

She came down the walk, carrying a battered cardboard box. "I'm sorry, Sam. I had no idea."

"No worries, little sis."

She thrust the box into his hands. "Last time I was up here, I found this in the closet of the guest room. I just gave it a quick look then. It's mostly Dad's stuff, but there might be a few things of Mom's in here, too."

"Does she know you're giving this to me?"

"No. Right now I'm so angry with her I don't really care."

Handing the box to Jana, he gave Maddie another hug. After putting the top up on the vehicle, he climbed into the driver's seat.

As he pulled out, Jana's fingers twitched on the box. "What do they say about curiosity and the cat?"

"We'll be home in less than an hour. You can wait that long." And he'd have that much more time to prepare for what new revelations might be inside.

Chapter Fourteen

Sam drove to his house, leery of the cozy intimacy of Jana's apartment. His stomach was still in knots, but he made them sandwiches anyway, mindful of Jana's need to eat for the baby's sake. They sat on the sofa, plates on their laps. He didn't touch his food, and she only nibbled at hers, both of them with one eye on the box they'd left on the coffee table.

"Go ahead," Sam said. "You might as well open it."

She set her plate aside. The tape across the top of the box was yellowed and loose, no doubt from Maddie's cursory inspection. Jana unfolded the flaps. The top of the box was high enough that she couldn't quite see inside, so she set it on the floor between them.

She looked up at him. "Do you want to—"

"You do it."

Jana started digging through, identifying each of her finds as she withdrew it. "A penknife. A sergeant's patch. Some army medals." She arrayed them on the coffee table.

"I didn't even know Dad was in the military."

"It would be cool to frame these. To show them to…" her hand dropped to her belly "…when he's old enough."

"Or she."

She gave him a sad, wistful smile, then reached into the box again. "What's this?"

She unearthed a painted wooden car from under a manila envelope. The garishly decorated seven-inch-long car tugged an old, old memory.

"My Pinewood Derby entry. From Cub Scouts." He took the lightweight pine car from her. "I was eight. It was my only year in Scouts."

During a rare, weeklong layover, his dad had helped him with the car, showing him how to sand it, helping him choose the paint. He'd brought home decals one day that Sam had plastered on the car from front to back.

"I can't believe he saved it." Sam had figured it was lost, like so much else from his early life.

Jana fished a business-size white envelope from the box. After she asked permission with a glance at him, she removed the contents.

On top was his dad's driver's license, its Commercial Class A rating allowing him to drive the big rigs. Taking it from Jana, he studied his father's photo, searching for some resemblance to his own face.

Jana brushed his arm. "Not everyone looks like both their parents."

He set the license on the table. "What else is in there?"

As she unfolded the two eight-and-a-half by eleven sheets in her hand, a square of cardboard fluttered to the floor. She picked it up absentmindedly, focused on the papers. "Your sister's birth certificate."

"The other one must be mine." His stomach did a dance as he considered whose name might be written under *father.*

Jana handed it over. His gaze scanned rapidly over the information. "His name is here. My dad's."

"Of course it is." She looked down at the card she'd dropped. "It's your mother's Social Security card."

He took it from her, reading his mother's married name, Linda Harrison, typed on the front. He had given Darius the name last week, but his friend had reminded him that someone with such a common name would be difficult to find.

But with his mother's Social Security number, Darius could probably track her down in a heartbeat. He placed the card carefully on the table.

Jana pulled a manila envelope from the box. Flipping the flap open, she slid out a photo. She turned it over, read the inscription. "Their wedding picture." She showed him the date. Four months before his birthday.

Okay, Aunt Barbara was right about that much. His mother was already in a family way on their wedding day.

The portrait of his parents, both of them smiling, happy for once, took his breath away. Again, he studied every feature of his father's face, searching for something familiar.

Jana looked over at him. "You are a dead ringer for her."

"I am," he agreed quietly. He supposed that ought to upset him. But he felt an odd sense of pride that he carried his mother's legacy in his face.

"But then, so is Maddie. Your sister has your dad's mouth, but the rest is pure Mom."

Jana's defense warmed him. She shook the remaining contents of the envelope out between them on the sofa. A half-dozen smaller envelopes fell to the cushions.

"I think they're letters," Jana said. "From your mother to your father, from your father to your mother." She stacked them neatly in date order. "The first one is from your mother. A month before the wedding date."

A sense of foreboding rolled over him as Jana placed the letter in his nerveless hands. He rose abruptly, knocking a couple of the other envelopes to the floor. "Be right back," he told her as he headed for the stairs.

In his room he lowered himself to the edge

of the bed. The letter might be completely in-
nocuous. A love letter. A pouring out of
youthful angst. A simple confirmation of the
pregnancy and of their plans to marry.

He separated the torn edges of the envelope
and extracted the sheet of pale pink paper.
Cautiously opened it flat. And read.

Tom,
You will always have my thanks for
getting me out of this fix I got myself into.
I promise I will be the best wife I can be if
you will only treat this baby as your own....

There was more, something about borrow-
ing a friend's car and a trip to Reno. He
barely took it in before dropping the letter to
the floor. His vision narrowed to that pale
pink sheet of paper between his feet as he
hunched on the bed.

He didn't even hear Jana come in. Barely

registered her picking up the letter and scanning it before laying it on the nightstand. It was only when she sat beside him and put her arm around him that whatever had frozen inside him started to thaw.

He was blind to everything but her—her warmth, the faint scent of honeysuckle, the silky feel of her hair when he brushed his mouth against it. At first he was only looking for comfort, but as he kissed her brow, then her cheek, her lips, a fire exploded inside him. All the sensual need he'd held at bay for the past several weeks burst through the barriers he'd used to confine it. He was helpless to deny it.

They fell to the bed, pushing clothes aside, unbuttoning and unzipping. When they were skin-to-skin, the swell of her pregnancy enthralled him, and he kissed and caressed every inch. He brought her to climax with his mouth and hands, then stood between her legs as she lay at the edge of the bed. With his arms propped on either side of her, he thrust inside her, feeling her belly against his, locking his gaze with hers. Reveled in the knowledge that this was *his* son or daughter inside her.

Afterward, they lay in bed together, her spooned up against him, his hand on that firm, rounded curve where the baby dreamed. His gaze fell on the letter on the nightstand. And with sudden insight, he knew what he had to do.

"Jana," he murmured before the fear could catch up with him. "I want to get married."

There wasn't an argument she could use to dissuade him. From that stubborn set to his face, Jana could see that Sam had his mind made up. He was ready to dig in his heels and wait for her to come around.

With the afterglow pretty much jolted out of her by Sam's pronouncement, she'd gotten up from the bed, tossed his clothes at him and pulled on her own. She marched from the bedroom and downstairs where her stale sandwich waited to satisfy her now-ravenous appetite. She was wolfing it down when he flopped next to her on the sofa, a just-try-me look on his face.

She sorted through all the reasons that marrying him would be a crazy idea, then settled on the one most important to her. "Why would I marry a man who doesn't love me? A man who doesn't even want me to love him. Unless that's changed?"

Even though he avoided a direct answer, she got the message anyway. "I'll be a good husband, a good father for our baby—"

"And what about that whole terrified-of-commitment story you told me last month? That's suddenly gone, poof?"

"Not exactly."

She saw it now, the same rigid control she'd seen in the shop the day she'd confessed her love to him. Fingers laced together in his lap, the tendons popping in his arms, the backs of his hands. The stiff set of his shoulders.

She set aside her empty plate and scooted herself away from him to rest against the arm of the sofa. It was all she could do to keep the tears from crawling up her throat. "Let me get this straight, then. You want to marry me, even though you don't love me, even though it scares the holy crap out of you, even though you don't have to, to make this child yours."

"My father did the right thing. I can, too."

Pain and anger and desolation built up inside her. She tried to grasp the emotions smashing around, to understand one clear thing. Then realization popped to the surface.

"I want you to love me, Sam. I want that to tie you to me, not obligation. Not 'the right thing.'"

"Marry me anyway," he said, his voice rough.

No was in her mind, on her lips even. But her throat wouldn't cooperate. It just wouldn't let enough air pass to speak the word. Not when he was sitting there, so close, his face so well loved, his scent, the memory of his touch still on her skin.

"Give me time to think about it," she said finally.

"Not too long."

Pulling her gaze from his, she bent awkwardly to find the shoes she'd slipped off earlier. He found them for her under the table and held her feet as he put them on for her.

"Could you take me home, please?" she asked.

"Tony and Rebecca are expecting us for dinner tonight."

"Tell them I can't make it."

They drove to the apartment in silence, Jana not taking an easy breath until Sam was gone. Maybe because she was so edgy, the baby was wide-awake, bouncing around like an Olympic gymnast.

Her brain was mush. There was no way she

could think this through clearly on her own. Frances was right downstairs, helping Ray run the shop, but no doubt the eighteen-year-old really wasn't up to having Jana dump her big-girl problems on her. No way could she talk to Tony, and Rebecca was probably way too busy in the ranch's bakeshop. Which left Estelle.

A quick call to the ranch told Jana that the former foster mother was up for a visit. Gathering up her car keys, she headed out, waving to Ray as he came out to dump some cardboard in the recycle bin. She made it to the ranch in record time and found Estelle out in the backyard of the main house, sitting in the pergola under the flowering wisteria.

In the cave of thickly blossoming wisteria, Estelle folded Jana into a big hug, then patted the seat of the bench. "It seems like months since we've talked."

Despite her smile, Estelle looked tired, her hands more puffy and swollen than Jana's own from her pregnancy. She felt a twinge of guilt for bringing her problems to Estelle when the older woman obviously wasn't feeling well.

"I know, I look like death warmed over," Estelle told her. "I'm fine. I just get a little tired when the weather warms up. Tell me what's going on."

Jana had intended to work her way into it, but instead she blurted out, "Sam wants to marry me."

Estelle beamed. "That's wonderful!"

"But he doesn't love me."

She thought maybe Estelle would argue the point, tell her, but of course he does. Except she didn't. She just said, "Sam has a tough time understanding what he feels."

"I do love him, Estelle. And he wants to be the father of my baby. I'd live sort of happily ever after." It was definitely one up on her mother, who never seemed to be able to get the men in her life to tie the knot. "But he made it pretty clear he'd only be marrying me out of obligation."

"He said that?"

It wasn't her place to reveal what Sam had just learned about his parents. "Let's just say he sees it as the right thing to do."

"So the question is, how can you be happy with that?"

"How can he?" Jana asked. "There'd be no more Shawnas or Cindys or Patricias. He'd be stuck with me."

"He's very fond of you." Estelle fixed her probing gaze on Jana. "But you don't think that's enough."

"I keep wondering, what happens in a few years? When I get some college under my belt and I don't have to depend on Sam for everything. When I can fend for myself, when he's not obligated anymore, what then? If he truly loved me, if he wasn't just *fond* of me, that'd be one thing. But if obligation is the only glue between us and then that's gone…"

Estelle didn't have an answer for that. So they sat there in the quiet of the backyard, concealed from the rest of the world by the wisteria, Jana's emotions as twisted as the vines overhead.

Then Estelle took her hand. "I think the real question, Jana, the one that really matters, is do you want to be a mother to this baby? Because marrying Sam is the only way to be sure of that."

Of course. Leave it to Estelle to lay it out so clearly. It spoke of her turmoil that Jana hadn't asked herself that very question before now.

"That is a no-brainer," Jana said. "Because all this time, when I've thought about giving her up, it's just about killed me. I love her already, more than I can even say. Despite the way she came about, despite her stinker of a father."

"Not anymore," Estelle reminded her.

"Because from this point forward, that father is Sam. Maybe he didn't put the baby there physically, but from the moment he took you under his protection, that baby was meant to be his."

As she spoke her piece, Estelle looked even more exhausted than she had when Jana had arrived. Jana helped the older woman to her feet and walked with her to the main house.

On the way to Sam's, she wrestled with second thoughts, third thoughts, an infinity of qualms and uncertainties. But the baby trumped every scrap of doubt, circling her back around to the same decision.

As she pulled up to his gate, it occurred to her that maybe she should have called him. For all she knew, he could be out. But as she pulled up to the house, she spotted him on the front porch, just coming around from the back.

He waited for her at the top of the steps, hands gripped at his sides. She climbed up, tipping her head back to look up at him, the expression on his face telling her he was filled with just as much misgiving as she was.

She said all she had to say. "Yes, I'll marry you."

He took her into his arms and held her for a long, long time.

Chapter Fifteen

With a waterfall of wisteria blooms as a backdrop, the mid-June Sunday sky so blue it made her heart ache, Jana whispered a shaky "I do" to Sam Harrison. He at least said his out loud, clear enough for the teens sitting in the last row to hear. His brief kiss barely qualified as one, his body so rigid she wondered if his tuxedo was stitched with two-by-fours. But they made it through with a passable imitation of a happy-to-be-wed couple.

Their quickie wedding had turned into a borderline monstrous affair with forty guests—twenty from the ranch alone, plus Sam's agent and publicist; his sister, of course; and even his housekeeper, Mrs. Prentiss. Because Sam wanted both Tony and Darius as best men, Jana had to have two bridesmaids also, so she asked Ruby and the ginormously pregnant Rebecca. Jana doubted anyone was looking at her. They were too busy wondering if Rebecca would pop before the ceremony was over.

Besides the expansion in the guest list, Rebecca's offer to have the kids prepare a light buffet brunch morphed into a catered sit-down that probably cost Sam some serious cash. The photographer Sam hired had just shot exclusive photos of some big celebrity wedding. Jana didn't want to see that bill.

By the time the paparazzo finished and the last of the receiving line tromped past, Jana's feet were killing her and her back screamed with pain. Not to mention the wedding dress that chafed around her middle because of her ballooning out the past few days since the fitting. Sam was beside her, his hand gripping hers a little too tightly, his forehead glistening with sweat in the hot sun.

When they finally relocated to the air-conditioned bakeshop dining room, Jana made a beeline for the head table and collapsed in a chair. Almost immediately Sam's publicist—a woman with a figure like a twig—hurried over.

The publicist waved her digital camera. "Could I just get one more shot of the two of you outside?"

"Later, Bridget. My wife needs a break." He all but shooed her away, throwing off his jacket and dropped into the seat beside Jana.

His hand cupped her cheek, turning her to face him. "It'll work out, Jana."

One way or another, she supposed. But would

things "work out" to keep them together? Without love as a tie? No point in asking those questions again. She'd made her bed.

He took her hand, running his thumb over the simple golden band he'd placed there such a short time ago. "I wish you'd let me get you a diamond."

"I don't like your history with fancy jewelry." Her joke came out harder edged than she'd intended. "I'm sorry. I'm tired, my feet hurt and my hands are swollen worse than Estelle's."

"The ring seemed like a tighter fit than I'd expected."

She wrinkled her nose at him. "Thanks for confirmation that I'm getting fat."

"It's not that. Your face seems…rounder. Swollen like your hands."

She wasn't about to mention the headaches. Sam would probably freak out, when it was just the stress of the wedding.

She made it through the rest of the reception by staying off her feet as much as she could. She and Sam kept their one dance brief; then she offered herself up to Tony and Darius. Sam waltzed gingerly with Rebecca, then Ruby, finishing with his sister, Maddie. Although Jana felt bad that Maddie had had to attend without her fiancé, she was grateful to have avoided an additional dance with Matthew.

Despite her best efforts to avoid it, Frances caught the bouquet and Ray the garter. The girl wouldn't even look at Ray after that, refusing his offer for a last dance.

When it was finally time to go, Jana changed into maternity slacks and blouse and carefully laid her wedding dress across the backseat of the Mustang. She wouldn't have even gone back inside except that she realized she'd forgotten her purse in the main house.

When she saw Tony, Rebecca, Darius and
Sam clustered around Estelle on the sofa, her
heart just about stopped. Estelle had had a
bad episode last year, shortly after Jana had
left the ranch. That she hadn't been here to
help was one more tick in the guilt column.

"Is she okay?" Jana asked. "What's going
on?"

Estelle was sitting up, but she looked
horrible—puffy and swollen, her breathing
coming in short gasps as if she couldn't get
enough air. She glanced over at Jana. "I'm so
sorry to spoil your wedding day."

"Never mind that." Sam gave his former foster
mother's hand a squeeze. "Darius and Tony are
going to take you to the emergency room."

Estelle didn't argue, which was pretty
scary in itself. Jana knew the older woman
hated hospitals.

Darius and Tony made a chair with their
arms and carried Estelle out to Tony's truck.

The two men climbed in with her and drove off, spitting gravel.

No one had the heart to toss rice at Jana and Sam as they made their way to the car. Already on an emotional razor's edge, Jana kept having to blink away tears as worry for Estelle tied her stomach up in knots.

Out of habit, she thought Sam would drop her off at the apartment. When he made the turn onto the road to his house, the realization that they were truly married dropped like a load of bricks. She wasn't going to be able to go back to her tiny apartment and crawl into her bed alone. To try to come to terms with whether she'd just made the biggest mistake of her life.

She didn't bother trying to fight the tears that spilled down her cheeks. Sam would assume she was crying for Estelle. And she was, but there was far more ripping her up inside. She'd had this crazy hope that once they spoke their vows, all her doubts would vanish. That she would be happy enough with the limits Sam had placed on their marriage. At least that it wouldn't hurt.

She kept her gaze out the window as they stopped at the gate to Sam's property. She was afraid to look at him, feared the rush of love that hurt so much inside. What should have been a day for tears of happiness just filled her with grief. Feeling sick to boot, her stomach aching a little from the rich food, just made her more miserable.

At least they wouldn't be doing that whole honeymoon thing, not yet anyway. Not with her pregnant as a hippo. They'd agreed to wait until the baby was born and old enough to leave with a sitter. The way she felt today, she wondered if she and Sam would last that long.

As he parked in the garage, in the fourth slot over, Jana turned to him finally. "Would you mind if I went in and took a nap? I'm beat."

He reached across to smooth a lock of hair behind her ear. "Not the wedding day you imagined, I'm guessing."

In a way it was, if you counted those days when she was twelve and thirteen, still dreaming that someday Sam Harrison would marry her. "It was beautiful. Thank you for everything."

He turned away, and she sensed all was not well in Sam Land either. Unable to bear one more scrap of anxiety, she climbed from the car and threaded her way through the garage to the house. After passing through the kitchen, she automatically turned right toward the guest room.

Sam's voice stopped her. "You're sleeping in my room now."

He didn't sound too sure of that himself. She glanced his way, taking in his troubled expression, and tried to smile, but her face felt too stiff. "I forgot."

As she walked past him toward the stairs, he followed just behind her. She wanted him with her, wanted him to go away and leave her alone. She wanted to feel normal again. That wasn't likely to happen for a while, certainly not before the baby was born.

While she pushed off her shoes and slacks, wriggled out of her short-sleeved blouse, Sam pulled back the covers for her. She crawled gratefully into the bed, rolling on her side with her back to him. Her arm curved around her bare belly, she felt the bump and grind of her little passenger who was really wearing out the welcome these days.

She'd started to drift off when she remembered Estelle. She raised her head from the pillow. "You'll wake me if you hear anything?"

"I will," Sam said, his voice sounding far away.

As she settled her head back down, she thought she heard the sound of a chair being pulled from the corner toward the bed. Then sleep had its way with her, dragging her into dreams.

Sam settled in the chair, nudging off his loafers and lifting his feet to the edge of the bed. He placed them carefully so as not to disturb Jana. She'd fallen asleep pretty quickly, not surprising considering the demands of the day, and the last thing he wanted was to wake her.

Hopefully she'd feel better by dinner. Mrs. Prentiss had insisted on making a light wedding supper as a gift for them. It was all packaged up in the fridge for later, salad ready to be tossed and main dish ready to be popped in the oven.

He didn't have an appetite, even though he'd been too keyed up to eat much from the wedding buffet. Considering his stomach still felt as if he'd eaten ground glass, he wasn't enthusiastic about whatever grudging labor of love the dour Mrs. Prentiss had prepared. Still, he'd eat it all with gusto if it put a smile on Jana's face.

He let his gaze trail down the lines of her body, the lightweight covers following its swells and curves. He doubted it was an accident that she'd turned her back to him. She'd been ready to go hole up in the guest room, likely would have if he hadn't said anything. Maybe he just should have let her.

He scrubbed at his face with his hands, trying to make sense of the stew of emotions inside him. He'd thought their marriage would throw a magic switch. That his fears would vanish, replaced finally with a sense of security. He would know that Jana was here to stay, that she and her child—their child— would forever be in his life.

But it hadn't worked out that way. Their I-do's raised more what-ifs than they'd answered. What if she stopped loving him? What if her heart couldn't bear his miserly, limited affection for her? What if she left him, just as his mother had? Except Jana wouldn't leave the baby behind. To have them both leave…

Despair battering him, he dropped his hands, drank her in, calming himself with the sight of her in his bed. But there was something even darker chewing at him, an insight into himself he didn't want to acknowledge. It wasn't Jana's leaving him he had most to fear. It was his leaving her.

The way his dad had left his mom again and again. Because even though he'd made the right choice, done the right thing, he found it impossible to live with it. So he picked a job that kept him far away from home, gave himself a legitimate way to escape the ramifications of the decision to marry Sam's mother.

Sam could do the same. He always got far

more requests for television interviews and
conference appearances than he accepted. He
could start saying yes more often, bring a laptop
with him to allow him to work on the road.
Jana wouldn't say a word, would accept him
putting his career first.

But when he thought of upping his travel,
spending lonely nights in hotel rooms in
Denver or Oklahoma City, the pain in his gut
just increased. Maybe his father had felt the
same way. Except in his dad's case, the scale
tipped more toward escape.

God, he needed to touch her. Even though
she'd shown her desire to keep her distance by
turning her back to him. He slid his feet from
the bed and walked quietly around it. He considered climbing under the covers but didn't
want to risk rousing Jana. So he lay on top, on
his side so he could face her.

Her hand was balled up at her face, her knees
bent up toward her belly. With slow movements

he shifted his leg to rest against hers, then laid his fingers lightly against her hand.

If this was all he had to do for the rest of his life—lying beside Jana, watching her sleep— maybe he could manage it. Except it was all so much more complicated. And he knew that if he didn't find a way to solve this riddle between his heart and hers, he would risk losing everything.

Two days after the wedding, Tony called with the latest news about Estelle. Jana recognized the caller ID as being from the ranch, but Sam got to the phone first. After a quick greeting, he said to Tony, "Hang on. Jana's with me. I want to put the call on speaker."

Then Sam reached for her, leading her to sit with him on the sofa. She held on to his hand so tight, she was probably making bruises.

"Estelle's got something called polycystic kidney disease," Tony said grimly. "She may have had it for quite some time."

"Polycyst—what does that mean?" Jana asked.

Tony's answer drifted from the handset. "Cysts have been growing in her kidneys, probably for years, replacing the good tissue. Her kidneys aren't functioning at all."

She glanced over at Sam and saw he looked just as scared as she felt. "So what are they going to do to fix her?" Jana asked. "They can make her better, right?"

"She'll have to have a kidney transplant," Tony said. "Which means we'll have to find a matching donor. Meanwhile, she's got to undergo dialysis several times a week."

"I want to get tested," Jana said. "To see if I'm a match."

"We all will," Tony said. "Darius is already contacting as many of Estelle's former fosters as he can."

After Sam hung up the phone, they sat on the sofa in each other's arms. Estelle's crisis should have brought them closer together—wasn't that part of being husband and wife? Except that even though Sam did all the right things—hold her, rub her back, murmur that everything would be all right—it almost could have been a scene he'd written in one of his books. He was still a million miles away from her, protecting his heart from the pain that losing Estelle would bring.

Jana sleepwalked through the next few weeks. She seemed to grow bigger on a daily basis, her feet swelling along with her belly and her hands, headaches keeping her awake at night. The doctor didn't like the way her blood pressure had crept up and pretty much restricted her to bed rest. The confinement made her feel only more crazed.

The news about Estelle was good and bad—good because she was responding well to the dialysis but bad because they hadn't yet found a match. It turned out that the rare set of antigens in Estelle's blood would make finding a compatible donor difficult.

Whether it was the problems with Estelle or Sam's buyer's remorse about marrying Jana, Sam kept to himself an awful lot. He'd hole up in his room, working until one and two in the morning. Jana saw him less than she had before they were married.

When he finally joined her in bed, she'd pretend to be asleep. That way, he would take her into his arms, snuggle up against her back. If he knew she was still awake, he would make sure not to touch her.

During those long hours alone, waiting for him to come to bed, hamster-wheel thoughts rolled around in her head. One minute she wanted to yell at him, shake him out from behind his iron bars. The next she wondered if she should just admit to him that their marriage was a big mistake. That they should part company now before the baby was born.

Then Sam would creep into the room, slip into bed beside her. Gather her up in his arms so tenderly that her heart would break into a zillion pieces. And she knew she couldn't leave even as she knew staying would tear her apart.

July arrived with a vengeance, slapping them with triple-digit heat on the first day. With nearly a month still to go before her due date, Jana woke on the third day of the heat wave feeling worse than ever. Her head pounded, her hands looked like the Pillsbury Doughboy's and she was crankier than a cartoon-deprived toddler. To top it off, Sam was as usual hiding in his office, working, even though it was a Saturday.

Restless and achy after breakfast, she stretched out on the living-room sofa, directly under the ceiling fan. Darius usually called on Saturday with an update on his search for Estelle's former fosters, so she had the phone at hand as she flipped through a baby magazine.

When it rang, she grabbed the portable, its

caller ID confirming it was Darius. "Hey, how's it going?" she asked.

"Is Sam there?" Darius asked.

Jana's anxiety bumped up a notch. "If it's about Estelle—"

"Estelle's fine. Nothing new to report. I'm calling about Sam's mother."

Prickliness danced across her skin. Sam had mentioned he'd finally given Darius his mom's Social Security number a couple days ago. Sam had told Darius to take his time, that the search for Estelle's fosters had top priority.

"Did you find her?" Jana asked.

"Let me talk to Sam," Darius said.

Sam must have sensed something, because he appeared at the top of the stairs. Jana waved him down, then handed him the phone when he came up behind the sofa.

"Yeah?" he said to Darius. He listened a while; then his face bleached of color. "Okay. Thanks."

Looking dazed and lost, he swayed, dropping the phone as he gripped the sofa back. Like a blind man feeling his way, he moved around the sofa, reaching out for Jana as he all but fell beside her. He pulled her into his lap, burying her head in his neck.

He shuddered, his mouth close to her ear. "She's gone, Jana. My mother is dead."

It shouldn't matter. It shouldn't mean a damn thing to him. His mother might as well have been dead the moment she walked out of their house twenty-five years ago. And yet it felt as if someone had run him through with a sword. Because somewhere deep inside, there was a little boy thinking he might see his mother again someday.

He started to shake, and before he knew it would happen, before he could stop it, he started to sob. It was coarse and ugly and had to be terrifying for Jana. He knew that deep inside. But he couldn't let go of her, because she was the only thing that mattered in his life, the only light that shone for him at the other end of this black tunnel he'd burrowed into. He just might die himself if he didn't keep his grip on her.

And she held on just as tightly, her fingers digging into the back of his neck, into his ribs. She murmured soothing sounds, comforting him just with her voice. That she loved him, that she would be with him always, that she would never leave him.

When he finally quieted, Jana's hair wet with his tears, his hold on her loosened, her hands relaxed against him. Yet she snuggled even closer, as much a part of him as his own self. And in that moment insight hit him with freight-train force.

He could never let her go. He would never walk away. She would be in his life for as long as he lived. Because he could trust her love, could count on it. Could rely on its constancy.

Whatever drove his mother to abandon him, that was about as foreign to Jana as antlers on a tiger. And his father's wanderlust had never rubbed off on him—he liked home base, liked the anchor and foundation of it. If he went anywhere, it would be with Jana and their child at his side. He didn't have to drag the shackle of his childhood anymore.

He would tell her. That the walls he kept between them had crumbled, that his heart burned now with a new passion. That from now on, their lives would be different.

"Jana," he whispered, his throat raw.

She leaned back from him, and for the first time he saw she didn't look right. "I don't feel good."

In the next moment she slumped in his arms, deadweight.

The next hour passed in a blur of panic. Calling 911, the excruciating wait for the

Advanced Life Support team—only ten minutes until arrival they'd told him, but it seemed forever. Then the controlled chaos as they worked over Jana—checking her blood pressure, starting an IV line, administering medication to bring down her high blood pressure, all the while in contact with the doctor at the hospital.

Jana had come to right after he'd hung up the phone, so he had that small comfort. But it broke his heart seeing her on the gurney as they rolled her from the house, IV line feeding into her arm and oxygen mask on her face.

He rode up front with the paramedic, lights and sirens clearing the way for the ambulance. Another agonizing wait, time crawling as they raced toward the hospital in Placerville. Everything seemed to move in slow-motion when they arrived, Jana pulled from the back, rushed inside and down the hall to Obstetrics.

Sam didn't like the look on the doctor's face when he checked Jana's blood pressure on the monitor. The man looked even more grim when he saw the baby's heart rate on the fetal monitor.

"The medication is not bringing your wife's blood pressure down, and your baby's in distress," the OB told him. "We have to do an emergency C-section."

Sam had no chance to react to the twin blows. They took Jana to the operating room while a nurse took Sam to change into scrubs. Panic surged again inside Sam—what if Jana died, like his father had, like his mother? What if he never had a chance to tell her he loved her?

He sat huddled in the OB waiting room, praying for Jana. He made deal after deal with God, if only He would let Jana and the baby be okay. He offered his own life if God wanted it, in exchange for Jana and the child she bore.

When the nurse appeared in the doorway, he jumped to his feet, taking in the woman's smile. "Are they okay?"

Her smile broadened. "Your daughter is in the Neonatal Intensive Care Unit, but she and your wife will both be fine. Would you like to see your daughter?"

Not even bothering to answer the no-brainer question, he followed the nurse to the NICU, then stared through the glass at the tiny bundle the woman pointed out. He could see only the scrunched-up face and a wisp of blond hair that poked out from the pink cap, but love poured out of him in a flood.

He didn't even realize his face was wet with tears until the nurse offered him a tissue. He hadn't cried in probably twenty years, and yet here he'd blubbered twice in one day.

"When can I see Jana?" he asked the nurse.

"Another half hour or so. I can come get you in the waiting room—"

"I'll wait here," he said, staring through the glass, beyond smitten.

Only the prospect of seeing Jana could have torn him away. As he stepped into the recovery room and saw her there, still connected to tubes but turning to him and smiling, his heart leapt into the stratosphere. Damn, he was crying a third time.

"I'm turning into a complete wuss, you know," he told her, swiping away the wetness. "All your fault. Yours and that little gem of perfection in there."

Jana's face glowed as if lit from within. "Isn't she gorgeous? I love her so much already."

"Me, too." He moved a plastic chair over to the bed and took her hand gently. "And I love you, sweetheart. In every way possible. As my wife, as my lover, as my friend. You've healed me, Jana. I want to spend the rest of my life repaying you for that gift. With my love."

Now tears shone in her eyes. He rose to kiss her cheek, to whisper every endearment he could think of into her ear.

The past faded, vanished, burned away by love and joy.

Epilogue

"Why a blindfold?" Sam asked, with daughter Sophie tucked on his hip, her brown eyes fixed adoringly on him.

"Because it's a surprise," Jana said, giving Sophie a noisy raspberry on her soft baby cheek. The five-month-old giggled, then returned her attention to the one who mattered most in her world—Daddy.

Jana wasn't the least bit offended that sweet Sophie was a Daddy's girl. Truth be told, the kid had both of them wrapped around her pudgy fingers. If Sophie could snap her fingers, she would, to order up whatever her heart desired in the moment—a piggyback ride on Daddy's shoulders, a snuggle with Grandma Estelle, or the quick appearance of the part of Mommy that Sophie loved best, Jana's breast.

Not that Jana would offer that up right now in the chill late-November air behind Celebration Station. She might have resigned herself to feeling like the family dairy, but even she had her limits.

"Stand still," Jana scolded as she reached up to tie the blindfold over Sam's eyes.

"Is this like the surprise you gave me at home while Sophie was napping?"

"In your dreams," Jana said. She pried her daughter from Daddy's arms—if the big lug tripped, she didn't want to risk Sophie's safety—and guided him through the shop's back door.

She held her breath as she and Sam moved slowly along the short hallway into the shop proper. This was what she'd spent much of Thanksgiving week doing, in between writing essays and reports for the two college classes she'd signed up for this semester. Frances and Ray had dropped in yesterday to help add the finishing touches, and with the shop closed today for Thanksgiving, she could finally show Sam.

They had to make their stop brief, with Tony, Rebecca, Estelle and the others expecting them for dinner at the ranch. The get-together would include not only all the students who had been through three sessions of Tony's independent living program but also Sam's sister and soon-to-be brother-in-law, Matthew, finally home from the Middle East.

They had a lot to be thankful for this year—their marriage, Sophie's birth, Matthew's safe return and the success of Celebration Station.

Although the doctors still hadn't found a compatible donor for Estelle, she was doing well enough with her dialysis treatment.

"Can I take it off now?" Sam asked.

"Hang on. Give me a sec." She raced around the room, flipping switches, pressing buttons. As the shop filled with light, little Sophie's mouth dropped open in awe.

Jana shifted her daughter to her other hip, mentally crossing her fingers. "Go ahead," she told Sam.

He shoved the blindfold off. Stared at what she'd done. His jaw dropped in such a perfect imitation of Sophie's expression that Jana started to rethink the whole nature-versus-nurture argument. Then he grinned at her and burst into laughter.

The shop was a riot of vivid color, a faithful copy of the magazine picture that had so enchanted him. Jana had decorated it with the wackiest and most outlandish Christmas symbols. A bunch of them were animated, and right now Santas and snowmen and penguins were ringing and dinging and singing with holiday cheer. Just like in the magazine, it was a child's fantasy of Christmas.

Sophie's head had swung around at the sound of Sam's laughter, and now the girl squirmed in her mother's arms, reaching for Daddy. Crossing the room, he lifted his baby girl up and held her against his chest.

He curved his warm hand against Jana's cheek. "Thank you for loving me. And thank you for giving me my family."

Looking up at him, Jana saw the devotion in Sam's eyes shining more brilliantly than any light in the room. She stepped into his arms, into the circle of his love.

* * * * *

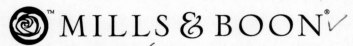